Fast Times at Spiro Agnew High

JAMES BLAKEY

Whitaker Lyon Press

Also by James Blakey

SUPERSTITION

THE CAT WHO LOVED DAVID
DUCHOVNY

Library of Congress Control Number: 2025902076

ISBN: 979-8-9909340-3-0 (paperback)

Whitaker Lyon Press
4464 North Point Drive
Broadway, VA 22815
WhitakerLyon.com

First paperback edition 2025

Contents

THE BICYCLE THIEF

2019 DERRINGER AWARD WINNER

No milk in the fridge, nor much of anything else.

Meant to hit the store yesterday, but stayed late grading papers. Afterward, a bunch of us TA's gathered at Stuffy's and closed the place.

My stomach rumbles. Off to find food.

Gray October skies. What happened to the sun? Gust of wind slams me in the face. I throw on a navy-blue hoodie.

I descend the fire escape, reach the ground, and stop.

Where my bicycle should be, there is only empty air.

***

Last night, too tired and tipsy to haul my bike up two flights. Locked it to a utility pole.

The chain lies on the ground, mocking me. I pick it up and rub my fingers over the deformed and broken link.

Small-town girl learns big-city lesson.

***

My bike.

They stole my bike.

This isn't some faceless crime, like distant Belarusian hackers cloning your debit card.

A real person, a horrible person, possibly someone I've smiled at while passing on the street, came to my home and stole it.

My bike.

Had it since sophomore year. Been with me through two moves and three break-ups. It's my transportation, my recreation, my freedom. It's a part of me.

And some jerk stole it.

My bike.

***

A call to the police proves worthless.

The city is engulfed in a crime wave. Four hundred murders this year, so far. A series of high profile car-jackings remain unsolved. Open air drug markets operate in view of elementary schools.

Law enforcement has no time for the degenerate who stole my bike.

***

The practical problem: come Monday, how am I getting to the university?

Hoofing it four miles, one-way, through The Borderlands, isn't an option.

Barely surviving on the grad-school stipend. Even resorting to UberPool would break me.

Not asking Jim. The last thing I want is a lecture.

Going to need a new bike. Well, new to me. The Norway vacation fund gets tapped again. Never going to see Tromsø during the Solstice.

My stomach grumbles. I settle for black coffee while browsing Craigslist for bikes.

***

I page through ads for mountain bikes, titanium frames, touring bikes, fat wheels, electric-assist bikes, hoping for something nearby and within my budget.

Who are these people who spend $4,000 on a used road bicycle? Wish I ha—Holy Hell!

A fire-engine red women's Raleigh Detour 2. Just like mine! Eight blocks away and asking fifty dollars. The listing is new, went up a couple of hours ago.

Could it be my bike? Impossible to tell from the photo.

Would the crook be that brazen? Or careless?
I reply to the ad and we arrange to meet.

***

Me: IN CASE I GO MISSING, I AM MEETING THE GUY FROM THIS AD AT 56TH AND MONTCALM
Me: CITY.CRAIGSLIST.ORG/BIKES/P5QR3322.HTML
Laura: WAIT, WHAT?

***

The seller's leaning against the gray metal shutters of New No. 1 Chinese Restaurant. Greasy hair. Empty eyes. Too thin for his clothes. Addict written all over him. Propped up against the bus shelter is the bike.

Not the bike. *My bike.* The mismatched handle-bar grips reveal its true identity.

This malefactor not only stole my bike, but he rode it with his dirty, smelly, drug-addled body.

If only my mind could kill him where he stands.

What to do? My heart thumps. Should have thought of a plan on the way over.

Accuse him? He'll just deny it.

Fight him? He's skinny, but still has thirty pounds on me. Plus, he's half-a-head taller.

Stall for time and hope a cop drives by?

I nod at the bike. "Why are you selling?"

"Girlfriend dumped me. She left it behind." He smiles at me. "I'm single now."

He has all his teeth. Heroin, not meth.

"Do you want it?" he asks.

"Let me take a look." I make a show of pretending to inspect my bike. "The tires are bald," I lie.

He doesn't glance at the bike and shrugs. "Okay, I'll take forty."

I kneel and run my finger along the chain. "The links are stretched. Chain is worn out." Another lie. Preventative maintenance is my religion.

How far can I talk down the price? Delusions of an O. Henry-esque conclusion, where the felon pays me to take my own bike, dance in my head.

"Who are you, Lance-fricking-Armstrong? Forty bucks!" He points a shaky finger at me. "Do you want it, or not?"

Perhaps I should have brought Jim. Don't the police ever patrol this street? I need a new plan.

"Let me try it out," I say.

"What?" He looks at me like I asked him to fly me to the Moon.

I stand up, putting my hands on my hips, and strike my best power pose. "I'm not going to buy a bicycle I haven't ridden."

He strokes his straggly chin hair. "Okay, but I'm gonna need a deposit."

"Deposit?" I shake my head. "It's a beater with bad tires."

"Nope. You have no leverage." He sweeps his arm through the air. "The city's full of buyers."

My eyes dart up the street. "Cops."

He takes the bait and turns.

In one swift motion, I grab the handlebars, hop on and pedal off.

My bike.

I have my bike. And I'm not giving it back.

I shift into high gear, rise off the seat and do my best impression of a Tour De France breakaway.

He's cursing a blue streak. Throws in the B-word.

I turn and grin. He's chasing after me.

My heart pounds. I hammer through the gears. He can't catch me.

I fly through a stop sign. A cab screeches to a halt. The driver honks and shakes his fist. I weave between a delivery truck and a transit bus, disappearing around a corner.

Above, the clouds part. Blue sky for the first time today. The sun emerges, bathing me in its golden rays, as I head home on *my bike.*

THE END

PORRIDGE

I'm in my office sorting a stack of bills higher than Rapunzel's tower, pondering which to pay and which I can stall. The radio announcer promises an update on a pair of missing kids, but first the weather.

The doorknob jiggles. I kill the radio. Hand on my Colt. Some creditors are more aggressive than others. The door opens. She's nineteen, twenty tops, in a patched and faded purple dress. Blond hair like it's spun from gold. Look up sapphire in the dictionary and there's a picture of those eyes.

"Mr. Pocopson?" Flat accent. Her *O*s sound like *A*s. Not from around here.

"That's me." I rise and shake her hand. Calluses. Short, unpainted nails. From the countryside? That would explain the purple.

"Ranja Brundqvist."

I remain standing until Ms. Brundqvist takes a seat. Mom drilled that one into me. Only thing she did right.

"Can I get you a drink? Coffee?"

She shakes her head, curls bouncing. "I wish to hire you, Mr. Pocopson. Last year, a friend of a friend, Red, had trouble with a stalker that you... handled."

Red's stalker was a wolf with big eyes and big teeth. Tracked him through the Enchanted Forest, got sloppy, and Wolfie had the drop on me. Looked like lights out until I jammed the barrel of the Colt in his big mouth. Forty-five caliber message delivered.

Ranja takes a deep breath, like she's screwing up her courage. "My younger sister Asta came to the city with dreams of being an actress. Life in Prairie Grove offered little for her. She emailed every week at first. But her messages became less frequent. An entire month went by and no word. I called, but her number's no longer in service. Her landlord claims she moved out three months ago."

"Have you gone to the cops?"

"I filed a report." Ranja waves her hand dismissively. "But the police aren't doing anything to find her. The ones who aren't openly corrupt are incompetent."

Give Ranja an A-plus in Civics.

"Will you look for her? I can pay." She drops two coins on my desk.

Copper. Prince Charming's smug mug on the obverse, pumpkin coach on the reverse. This won't even fill up my truck.

"Ms. Brundqvist, I'd like to help, but an investigation of this sort isn't cheap." I hand back her coins. "Probably your sister's fine. Caught up in the thrill of living in the big city."

"How silly of me. I should have known." Ranja's holding back tears as she stands. But her knees buckle, and she collapses in the chair. Hands covering her face, she sobs.

I hate it when they cry.

I offer a tissue. "I can poke around for a day."

She blows her nose. Looks at me with those blue eyes. "Thank you."

"Do you have a photo?"

Ranja hands me a five-by-seven. Same sapphire eyes. Hair so bright, I need to squint. And a smile that reminds me of Hannah's. I can understand why Asta wasn't satisfied with life on the farm. One good thing about this case: People will remember her.

"Did Asta talk about any friends that she'd made, perhaps men?"

Ranja shakes her head. "She mentioned no one."

"Did she have a job?"

"She wrote she landed a gig doing dinner theater at The Poisoned Apple."

Ranja notices my expression. I need to work on my poker face.

"You've heard of it?" she asks.

"Yeah, I know it." My ex owns the joint.

The girls who work there aren't doing dinner theater.

***

The Poisoned Apple sits between an alchemical plant and the stockyards in a section of the city so far from gentrification you couldn't find it with a magic mirror. The stench alone is enough to keep away all but the most debauched.

I pull into the unpaved parking lot filled with ten-year-old work vans and pickups. The club is two stories, brick, no windows. On the roof, a neon red sign flicks between an apple and an apple missing a bite.

A grumpy dwarf, nose as big as an eggplant, is the muscle working the door. I show him the photo of Asta. He growls, face as red as his tunic. Doesn't know her. Tells me to ask Butcher.

Inside I find the typical Friday night crowd. Enchanted frogs arguing with wisdom-dispensing owls. Tin soldiers drinking away their sorrows and pay. The Three Pigs, fronted by The Pied Piper, jam a rockabilly cover of "Be Our Guest." Atop six-foot platforms, girls in tiaras, glass slippers, and not much else gyrate to their own beat inside upright crystal coffins.

Butcher's standing on a riser behind the bar, spectacles thick as whisky tumblers, gray hair peeking beneath his green tuque. Even when we were in the service, he always managed to wear that hat.

I flash Asta's picture. "Seen her around?"

"Hell, Pocopson. Drink an order, uh, order a drink. We're running a business here."

I drop a coin on the bar. "Scotch. Not that bilge you keep under the counter. The real stuff."

Butcher disappears into the back and returns with my drink. He peers at the photo. "That's Goldilocks."

"Her name is *Asta*."

Butcher shrugs. "We give dakes to all the fancers. I mean fakes to all the dancers. Protects their privacy."

"Your concern for the well-being of these young ladies is touching. When's the last time you saw her?"

Butcher scratches his head. "A week ago? Last Friday, maybe Thursday?"

"And you weren't concerned that she hasn't showed since?"

"No big deal. Dancers drift out and in. In and out."

"Any patrons show particular interest in Goldilocks?"

"Too busy to keep tabs." Butcher gestures to the line waiting for drinks.

"Keeping tabs is your job." The joke is lost on him. "Would the boss have any idea?" I want to avoid her, but Butcher's no help.

"Flutter!" Butcher shouts.

Flutter has his back to us, washing glasses in the sink. Butcher slaps him in the head so hard his purple cap flies off. Butcher signs to go upstairs and ask if she'll see me.

"It might be a while," Butcher says. "Want some food?"

I order a plate of wings and a beer. Kingdom News Network (KNN) is muted on a high-def crystal ball mounted over the bar. Volunteers lock arms and march across a meadow. The scroll reports The Royal Family is offering a reward: one hundred gold coins for information leading to the safe return of Hansel and Gretel Lofgren.

I almost crack a tooth on a wing. Not a bone. The damn thing is frozen. Perfect match to the warm beer.

I turn my attention to the crowd. A tipsy miner collides with a drunken woodcutter, spilling his drink. Voices rise. Glasses shatter. Fists fly. The woodcutter's getting the worst of it. A pair of dwarves lock onto the miner's legs, but that doesn't slow him down. Two more dwarves join in, swarming the miner, knocking him off balance. He crashes to the floor.

"Heigh-Ho! Heigh-Ho! It's to the street you go!" The four diminutive bouncers hoist the miner over their heads, carrying him out the club.

Flutter's back. He signs: she will see you now.

***

Mirrors cover the walls of Snow's office. For as long as I've known her, she's surrounded herself with them. Vanity? A way of processing trauma? Both?

It's been two years, but she looks better than ever, leaning against her desk with a smile that belongs in a toothpaste commercial. Hair black as an evil queen's heart. Lips red as a freshly waxed sports car. Skin white as—well, you know.

Blue puffy sleeves must be out. Snow's dressed in all black: low-cut blouse, micro-skirt, fishnets, knee boots. The contrast against her skin is... enough to make me forget why I'm here.

"You're looking well, Timmy." Snow's the only one I let call me that.

She reaches to hug me. This meeting could quickly go horizontal in more ways than one. I dodge the embrace, grab her hand, and kiss her knuckle.

This satisfies her, lips curling into a demure smile.

"Why are you here, *Timmy?*" She says my name like a schoolteacher lecturing a naughty second-grader. "Ready to give up chasing deadbeat wizards and cheating royals for a steady paycheck?" Snow does that thing where she arches one eyebrow. "I'm opening a new club: The Spinning Wheel. But I need someone I can trust to run it."

I shrug. "You've got seven candidates downstairs."

"The dwarves are competent." She sighs. "Six of them, anyway. But they lack a certain ruthlessness that management in our industry requires."

"I'll consider it." My chest tightens. I don't enjoy lying to Snow, but no way I'd work for her. I pull Asta's photo from my pocket.

"Oh, yes, I know this one. Gold—Goldilocks. Really packs them in. What's your interest?"

"*Asta's* been missing for a week."

"Missing?" From her tone, she didn't know.

"I see you're on top of the personnel as well as Butcher is."

Snow shrugs. "Another reason I need a club manager."

"When Asta was packing them in, did anyone show an unusual amount of attention?"

"Sure, but what's in it for me?" Snow smiles again, but this time it's not demure. More like a lioness about to feast on dinner. She steps into my personal space, scent like a peach orchard in the summer. She fiddles with my collar, fixes her gaze on me. Everyone raves about Snow's skin, but for me, it's always been about her eyes. Tiny brown circles around the pupils, then a ring of amber, and finally green.

She loops her arms around my neck, pulls herself closer. Her lips brush my ear. She whispers, "Perhaps we can work out a trade." Snow kisses me, tongue exploring my mouth.

I kiss back, instinctively, reflexively, wrap my arms around her. I miss this, her, us. After ten seconds, I remember how it always ends. I push her away.

"That's no way to get my help." She waves her hand dismissively. "You can leave."

I stand my ground. "I'm the one doing you a favor."

She crosses her arms. "How magnanimous of you."

"If The Poisoned Apple gets the reputation for dancers disappearing, you'll have a tough time replacing them. That's bad for business. People don't come for the food."

Snow laughs. "The Apple has the exact reputation I want. We didn't skip a beat when Goldy wandered off. There's an infinite supply of cute peasant girls who trek to the city hoping to strike it big. When things don't work out..."

No cards left. Time to bluff. "You don't realize who Asta is. Her aunt spends summers on the North Shore with *Cindy*. That's how she put it. Besties with the Princess. The aunt wants the inquiry handled discreetly. If I don't make progress, she'll call the authorities. You want a parade of health inspectors marching through the club every night? All your dancers have their working papers? And good luck with the permits for your new place."

Snow studies me with those eyes, deciding to call or fold. "Fine, I'll do my civic duty. There was one imp who took an interest in Goldilocks."

"You got a name? Or do I roust the whole damn city?"

"No name. Nobody knows it. The one with the reputation for making one-sided deals."

"Let me guess. He hasn't been around since last week."

She shrugs.

"Snow, did you bother to warn Asta about the imp?"

"She's an adult, Timmy. We're all adults."

That's why Snow and I never worked out. She doesn't care about anyone but herself. The real reason her stepmother went after Snow? She couldn't stand that they were so much alike.

"Thanks for the info."

"When you're done playing White Knight, stop back and we'll *chat*."

"Sure." Not certain which is worse, seeing Snow again or lying to her.

***

Years ago, a couple of rival princes fell for the same mermaid. The Kingdom restarted the draft, because royal puppy love is a matter of national security. My number came up, and they shipped me to the front. No one to watch out for Hannah. Even as I told Ranja I'd only spend a day looking for Asta, I knew I wouldn't stop. Someone has to protect little sisters.

I work my way through the worst of the West End, following the imp's wake of frauds and swindles. No need for fists or payoffs. The victims are eager to tell their stories. But no one knows where to find him until a cat in the finest looking boots tips me to a spot down by the docks.

Kitty was correct. I find the imp at the end of an alley, standing atop a garbage can. He's a meter tall, orange hat like a traffic cone, scraggly black beard. The imp's talking with a sailor in his dress whites. Rats gather in a circle, enjoying the conversation.

The sailor's voice cracks with doubt. "I have to give up my first-born?"

"She'll be the love of your life. Can you feel that hole in your heart? It will never heal until you two are together," the imp goads him. "I'll also ensure you're promoted to officer, command your own ship."

The sailor wavers. "Okay, I gu—"

"Get out of here!" I grab him by the shoulders. "You don't want this."

"But I do." Tears in his eyes.

I slap his face. "Not this way. He feeds off your hope. Exploits your heartbreak. You want this girl? Find a way to make it work without his help."

The sailor blinks, like he's waking from a slumber. "You're right." He points a finger at the imp. "Deal's off!" He stumbles up the alley to the street.

I grab a trashcan lid, slamming it against the brick wall. "Scram!" I yell at the rats.

They oblige, chittering as they scurry away.

"Not very neighborly scaring off my customer and friends," the imp says.

I pull out Asta's photo. "Seen her around."

"I know her." The imp grins with crooked, jagged teeth. "Let's talk a bargain for her location. What ab—"

I grab him by the collar and lift. His legs pinwheel, kicking at me.

"Do I look like I fell off the sugarplum boat? Where is she?"

The imp says, "Let me give you some unsolicited advice. Leave her be. The girl's a psycho. Caught her snooping through my phone."

Holding him with my left hand, I deliver a right across his jaw.

Blood trickles from his lip. "Once made a bargain with a prize-fighter. He would win every bout, but promised me his true love. When she came al—"

I deliver another right. "I don't want to hear anything, except where I can find Asta."

"*Asta*?" He cackles. "You must have it bad for her. Here's the deal, Sport. You can beat me, kick me, torture me. I'll never tell. This—" he wipes the blood from his lip with his hand, holds it up "—is kid's stuff."

I stare into his eyes, brown as coffee beans. The imp's telling the truth. I can't knock the info out of him. While I'd enjoy beating him on principle, revenge for everyone he's used and tricked, I need to focus on finding Asta.

"What kind of deal you offering?" I ask.

"Excellent." He stares back at me. No, more like staring inside me. "No loves. No prospects. No family. Forget about kids. Not even a pet. What an empty life."

I shake him. "This is about her, not me."

He grins. "You *do* have something of value. Integrity. It's been decades since I collected on that."

My arm is getting tired. I drop him on the lid. "How does this work? Do we need a notary? Sign in blood?"

"Nothing so dramatic. A verbal agreement will do. I'll provide the info to find the girl. Once you retrieve her, I get your integrity." He rubs his hands together. "How I enjoy dropping you holier-than-thou types down a few pegs."

"If that's what you see in me, you're mistaken."

"I know your kind. Think you're better than all of us. Living up to your personal code. A monologue filled with strained metaphors running through your head. I'm going to enjoy taking this from you.

"Afterward, you'll look and sound the same, but you'll be hollow inside. Your friends, the people who depend on you? You'll betray them at the drop of a hat. For no other reason than because."

I say nothing, glaring at him.

"There's an escape clause. You get three chances to guess my name. Do that and you keep your integrity. Do we have a deal?"

I furrow my brow and stroke my chin like I'm struggling with the decision. "Deal."

"Excellent." The imp raises his hand. "I'll st—"

"Rumpelstiltskin!"

"What?" His face white as Snow's.

"I'm cutting through all the nonsense. Your name's Rumpelstiltskin." Been holding this ace in my back pocket for years. "Where is she? Don't think of backing out or everyone will know your name. I'll spread it all over the Kingdom. In every newspaper, every subreddit."

His face contorts in horror. "Don't do that."

"Not much fun when you're on the short end? Tell me what you know."

"That girl is more trouble than she's worth. Goldy was using."

"What did you hook her with?"

"Wasn't me." He holds up his hands in a sigh of surrender." "She was on the Porridge before we met."

"Porridge?"

"Bears, the *Tribus Ursis*, push it. The ultimate high, the most unfathomable downer, or the perfect chill. Not that I've used the stuff." He hops to the ground and heads up the alley.

He gets three steps before I horse collar him.

The imp twists, trying to break my grasp. "Hey, I'm not going anywhere. I want you to see something by the curb."

Little plastic baggies litter the gutter. I inspect the bags: logo of a bowl. Labels read too hot, too cold, and just right.

"These bears know where she is?" I ask.

Rumpelstiltskin nods. "Last time I saw her, she was going to their cottage in the Enchanted Forest. I'll draw you a map."

***

My truck's undercarriage scrapes gravel. Must be ten years since they graded this fire road. I'm bringing my shotgun and a pack of cold weather gear for my expedition into Bear Country. The radio is predicting a blizzard: high winds and twenty-five centimeters of snow.

Branches scratch the sides of the pickup. The road narrows, becomes a path. I get out, load up, and check the map. The bears' house looks to be another five klicks.

Couple of centimeters of old snow on the ground. Clouds blanket the sky. Wind picks up. After an hour, I should be close. But the map's all wrong. No sign of the rock chute that marks the halfway point. Or the two streams I should cross.

Either Rumpelstiltskin sucks with maps, or he lied. I'll push on another half hour. If no house, it's back to the city and make that imp wish he'd never met me.

Fifteen minutes later, I smell burning wood. In a clearing stands a cottage. Lights on. Smoke rising from the chimney. I crouch at the tree line, watching through my binoculars. The siding looks like gingerbread. And the shingles? Are those Rice Krispy treats?

I cross the lawn, peer through a window. Frost covers the glass. I try to wipe it away. No luck. I put a finger to my tongue. Not frost. The panes are made of sugar. Inside, a figure is moving. It's not a bear. This isn't the place. Maybe whoever's inside can direct me to *Tribus Ursis.*

Shotgun broken open and over my shoulder, I knock on the door (white chocolate?). A redhead answers. She wears a green flowing gown. Around her neck hangs a silver necklace with a crystal pendant. She flashes a smile that makes me feel like I'm floating. Her slim fingers stroke the pendant. A black cat meows and rubs against my leg.

"Can I help you?" she says.

I can't remember what I want to ask. Or why I'm here. Even my name is fuzzy.

She grabs my hand. "Let's get you out of the cold."

The house is warm, smells like a flower garden. I want to take a nap.

"Help!" a girl cries.

"What's that?" I slap myself across the face, fighting the urge to close my eyes.

"Just the radio." The redhead caresses my shoulder, and I want to sleep for a hundred years.

"Help!" This time a boy's voice.

My knees are wobbly. My head spins. I'm falling. Arms out, my hand shatters a sugarcane windowpane. The blast of cold air stirs me from my daze.

I stand, re-invigorated, snap the shotgun closed, aim at the redhead.

Her fingertips crackle with electricity. "Men aren't as tender as children, but I'll feast on your leftovers all winter." Bolts of energy shoot from her hands, blasting the shotgun from my grasp.

I dive for the floor, roll, and come up with the Colt. Fire one shot and hit her in the shoulder. She screams. Blood covers her gown.

I dash toward the cries for help. On a table in the kitchen, a boy and a girl trussed up in a giant roasting pan.

The missing kids!

Pulling a knife from my pack, I slice away their bonds.

An electric bolt strikes the pan, sends it flying. I flip the table, use it as a shield. The kids crouch next to me. I shoot again, miss. The witch retreats behind the doorway.

I grab the pan, fling it, break a window. Cold air rushes in. I tell the kids next time I shoot to scramble out the window. Follow my tracks to my truck and the road out the forest.

I give Hansel my keys. Gretel hugs me. I fire at the doorway, splintering the jam. The kids clamber out the window.

Three bullets left. The wind calms. The flower garden scent fills the room. I fight the urge to yawn.

"Tim?" Hannah's voice.

My mind's fogging up. Must be a trick. I pinch myself.

"I knew you'd come for me," Hannah says.

"You're not real!" I need to get out of here. Try to stand, but the room spins. I fall to my knees.

"I'm real as you need me to be."

I peer over the table. Hannah steps into the doorway. Same blue dress as the day I shipped out.

"How is this possible? You're dead."

She smiles at me. God, I missed that smile.

"I've been hiding in the woods. I always knew you'd rescue me." She crosses toward me.

I want this to be true. I want it to be her. It's hard to think, like my brain is molasses.

Hannah hasn't aged a day since I last saw her.

Deep in my mind, an alarm goes off.

"Hannah, how can you still look like this?"

"The witch cast a spell. A favor while she hid me."

"Stop!" I point the gun at her.

"Tim, what are you doing?" She holds up her hands.

Not Hannah. A trick.

I hope.

I thumb back the hammer.

"I'm sorry," I whisper, then unload the last three rounds into her chest. Hannah's face is a mix of horror and shock. Her dress explodes in red. She falls to the floor.

The cat is nuzzling the body. Not Hannah. Not the redhead. An old woman. Wispy gray hair. Empty black eyes filled with death.

My mind is clearing. I step over the body, grab the shotgun in the next room, and rush outdoors.

Wind is gusting now, blowing snow, filling my tracks. After five minutes, I lose the trail. I continue in what I think is the right direction. When I'm certain I'm lost, I climb a ridge to get my bearings.

From the ridgeline I spot a house down the valley. Wooden, one floor, needs paint. The door opens. Three brown bears rumble out. No Asta. They're heading toward the opposite ridge. I follow them with the binoculars, watch them disappear over the slope.

I race to the cottage and pound on the door. "Hello?"

No answer.

I push my way inside. Steam rising from bowls on the dinner table. Why'd they leave without finishing their meal? More importantly: when are they coming back?

In the living room, plastic baggies and a scale sit on a table. Broken wood litters the floor. Looks like someone smashed a chair. Was there a fight?

"Asta?" I call out.

Muffled sounds from the next room. I slip through the door. Three beds. The closest two are empty, but they've been slept in. Lazy bears, not making your beds. In the third, someone is hiding under the covers.

"Asta?" I pull back the blanket.

Pale clammy skin, bloodshot eyes. Dull matted hair. Hard to believe it's the same stunner in the photo.

"Wh—Who are you?" she asks.

I pull the covers all the way off. She's dressed in a t-shirt and shorts. Veins marked up. I help her stand, but she's shaky. "Can you walk, or do I need to carry you?"

"Carry me where?"

"Home. Your sister's waiting for you."

"Ranja?" Her eyes are glazed, lost. "But I like it here."

"Not going to argue."

Pair of sneakers beside the bed. I slip them on her feet. Stuff the shotgun in my pack, dress her in my coat. I carry her out the house—at least she's light—trudging up the incline. No idea where to find my truck and the fire road.

Roars from behind me. The bears are on the far ridge. Didn't think they had good vision. Maybe they smell me?

"We have to run." I set down Asta, hold her hand, and we're off.

She's stumbling, but I keep her upright. We make it to the woods. Now what? We can't outrun them. Climb a tree? They'll wait us out.

A hundred meters into the woods, we crouch behind a downed log. The bears are racing through the forest. I pull out the shotgun. Can't hit them at this distance, but I can scare them. I fire a barrel over their heads.

"All I want is the girl!" I shout. "I don't care about the drugs!"

The bears stay out of range. The smallest stands his ground while the bigger two circle us. If they attack simultaneously, our position is indefensible.

I grab a plastic spray bottle and a box of ammo from my pack. I reload the Colt, hand it to Asta. "Use this to protect yourself."

The gun slips from her hands. "Baby Bear, help me!"

"I'm coming, Asta," the small bear shouts. *Small!* That cub must weight a hundred-and-fifty kilos.

Baby rushes toward me, while his parents yell for him to wait. He hurdles the log, and I deliver a blast of bear spray in his eyes.

He screams, covers his face, rolls on the ground.

"What did you do to my son?" Mama Bear bounds toward me.

I fire a round from the shotgun. Hit her in the front leg. She roars, but comes no closer.

A growl from behind. I turn, and a paw slaps the shotgun from my hands. Papa Bear strikes again, sends me flying. My leg snaps as I strike the ground, looks like I have a second knee. Blood trickles in my eyes. The shotgun is beyond my reach. I try crawling. My leg erupts in pain.

Papa slams me in the jaw. I can't even plead for him to stop. Never thought it would end this way.

Gunshots explode. Papa Bear halts, a look of surprise on his face. More shots, and he collapses. Did Asta stop him with the Colt? Doesn't seem possible. I try to wrestle myself up, but fall backward.

"Take it easy."

Snow?

I blink through the blood. She's dressed in a black parka and ski pants, holding a rifle, flanked by Butcher and Flutter.

"Take your son and go." Snow raises the rifle at Mama Bear. "Or stay and die."

Mama growls, but she and her blubbering baby wander off.

"This will make a nice rug for my office." Snow kicks Papa's lifeless body. "Butcher, see to Timmy."

Butcher served as a combat medic in the Mermaid War, does a quick evaluation. "Contusions, broken jaw, and a compound fracture of the tibia. He'll live."

"What about her?" Snow points at the shivering Asta.

"Withdrawal," Butcher says.

I try to speak, but my jaw won't move. I sign: what are you doing here?

Butcher says, "The thoss bought—I mean the boss thought you could use some help."

That's the last I remember, before I pass out.

***

Two weeks later, and I'm starting to heal.

Turns out Snow ordered Flutter to follow me when I left The Poisoned Apple. When he reported I was heading into the Enchanted Forest, Snow and Butcher loaded up all firepower they could carry and raced to save my butt. I misjudged Snow. She cares about people. Or at least me. She's nursing me back to health. Maybe we have a future. But I still won't work for her.

Rumpelstiltskin skipped town. Heard he set up shop on one of the Seven Isles. I might have to write an anonymous letter to the authorities there.

Hansel and Gretel stumbled through the woods to my truck and drove to civilization. They told their story to the authorities, who ruled my killing the witch was self-defense.

Ranja took her sister to a top rehab clinic in the tropics. Those places don't come cheap, but it's the best bet for a full recovery. I used the reward to cover her stay. Have to look out for little sisters. What else was I going to do with the money?

Pay some bills?

THE END

BOTTOM OF
THE
THIRTEENTH

"What happened to Eddie?" I stood in the warehouse parking lot ready for my weekly run up North.

"Eddie retired," said the man with dark eyes. "I'm Paolo. I run things now."

"What's that mean for me?"

"Relax, kid." Paolo smiled to show crooked teeth. "I'm giving all his people a chance to audition."

"Great, Eddie had me t—"

Paolo held up his hand. "I have my own ideas about the audition. You're going to drive the rabbit."

"Rabbit? Like an old Volkswagen?"

He chuckled. "This is the rabbit." He pointed to a tan Camry with Florida plates.

"What am I hauling?"

"Nothing."

"Huh?"

"One of my people will do the transporting. Your job is to drive eighty-five, ninety on the Interstate in front of him and flush out any cops."

"You want me to get pulled over?"

He nodded. "You'll be reimbursed for any tickets."

"Where am I headed?"

"Wilmington."

"Delaware or North Carolina?"

"Delaware." He gave me a flip phone. "If my guy has to stop, he'll text you. You get pulled over, you text him."

"What if I have to take a leak?"

"Hold it or use this." Paolo handed me an empty twenty-ounce Powerade bottle. "Prove yourself and there's a spot for you in my organization."

"When's the trip?"

"Ten minutes."

"Ten minutes? But I need to pack and g—"

"No, you don't. Operational security. Got your license with you and enough cash for gas to Delaware and back?"

I nodded.

"Then you're all set."

***

One of Paolo's lieutenants gave me a bag of McDonald's and a map. My path was highlighted: I-85 north out of Atlanta to I-95 in Virginia, around the DC Beltway to US 301 over the Chesapeake, and up the Eastern Shore to Wilmington.

Outside of Atlanta the radio was nothing but country, country and more country, until I found the Braves playing the Giants. I set the cruise control for ninety, passing through South Carolina without incident. Beyond Charlotte I got a text telling me to pull over. I filled up and grabbed a two-liter of Mountain Dew and a couple of Hostess cherry pies, the kind with the sugar-coated crust.

Nearing midnight, I crossed into Virginia. The Giants rallied to tie in the ninth. Pressure built on my bladder. I grabbed the empty Powerade bottle. Do truckers execute this maneuver while driving? I pictured the logistics in my mind. That only made the pressure worse.

Bottom of the thirteenth, the Giants had men on second and third with one out when red-and-blue lights flashed in my rearview mirror.

I texted: COPS PULLING ME OVER. I powered off the phone, stopped on the shoulder, and rolled down the window.

Troopers approached on both sides shining their flashlights into the car.

"Sir, can I see your license, registration and insurance, please?"

Cursing myself for not asking Paolo about insurance and registration, I fumbled open the glove compartment, found the papers and handed them and my license to the trooper.

"Mr. Case?" He shined the flashlight in my eyes.
"Yeah?"
"Who is Dominic Gutierrez?"
"Who?"
"The registered owner of this car."
"Oh, yeah, that's my cousin. He lent me the car."

"Do you have any illegal substances or weapons in the vehicle, Mr. Case?"

I shook my head. "Nope."

"Then you won't mind if we search the vehicle?"

I shrugged. "Not at all."

I stepped out of the car, and the trooper instructed me to place my hands on the hood.

"Nothing," said the partner after the search.

"Told you," I said.

"How about popping the trunk, Mr. Case?" asked the first trooper.

"Sure." I slipped the keys out of my pocket and stepped toward the back.

He put his hand on my chest. "I'd prefer to open it myself."

"Whatever."

The trooper took the keys and headed to the back of the car. The trunk lid lifted up, blocking my view. The troopers said something, but I couldn't make out what.

Both approached me with serious looks on their faces and hands on their weapons. The first trooper slammed my head against the hood.

"Hey! I—"

"Shut up!" he roared. "You're under arrest." He grabbed my wrists, handcuffed me, and dragged me to rear. As he stuffed me into the patrol car, I caught a glimpse of the open trunk.

There lay Eddie with lifeless blue eyes and a gunshot wound in his forehead.

THE END

THE CRISP-R CONNECTION

"Destination reached," the GPS announces.

Vito maneuvers the Lincoln into the unpaved lot next to a softball field. Late model Accord in the far corner, near the concessions stand, parked under the sole streetlight. Too dim to make out the color.

The Lincoln bounces toward the car. Need to get new shocks. Vito parks fifty feet away, high beams on the Honda. He slides open the window. Dry wind blowing down the desert. He twists his head left, then right. No one else around.

Vito slips on a pair of surgical gloves, struggles to get an N95 respirator into place. He gets out, taps the Glock in his shoulder holster, strides toward the Honda.

A kid—twenty-five, Dodgers long-sleeved t-shirt, needs a haircut—leans against the driver's door, lost in his phone.

Vito stops ten feet away, clears his throat.

The kid giggles at his phone, doesn't look up.

"Hey!" Vito's voice, full of malevolence, cuts through the mask and the wind.

"Huh?" The kid's startled, drops his phone, goes to grab it.

"Freeze!" Vito pulls out the Glock.

The kid stops, bent over, like an upside-down capital L.

Vito says, "Stand up, slowly. Then back away from the car."

"It's kind of hard to hear you through that mask."

Vito shouts, "You won't have trouble hearing anything ever again if you don't back up!"

The kid straightens, takes one shaky step backward. "Sure, but wh—"

"No talking." Vito waves the gun. "Keep moving."

When the kid's twenty-five feet away, Vito motions him to stop. Vito peers in, around, and under the car. No one. No weapons. He grabs the phone, new Samsung, and slips it in his pocket.

The kid says, "What are you doing? I still have four paymen—"

"After our business is concluded, you can have it back," Vito says. "You the one with CRISP-R?"

"Yeah, I'm Bra—"

"Christ! No names. Where's the stuff?"

"Got it in the trunk."

Vito's eyes flick to the car. Sweat breaks out on his forehead. He licks his lips and takes a step back. "That safe?"

The kid shrugs. "Why wouldn't it be?"

Vito, with the Glock pointed center mass, says, "Slowly take out your keys and toss them over."

Vito catches the keys, double clicks the fob. The trunk pops.

"What do you think?" The kid beams like a first grader with a perfect report card.

Vito squints. Bunch of plastic trays. Some clear. Others white. "What the hell is this?"

"Crisper drawers. Keeps your fruits and veggies farm fresh. I got all the major brands: Frigidaire, Whirlpool, Kenmore."

"This a joke? I want the thing that slices and dices DNA. You do work for ChromosomoCorp, don't you?"

A look of pride crosses the kid's face. He stands straighter, puffs out his chest. "Sure, I run their Twitter account."

"Twitter?" Vito feels the acid eating away at his stomach lining. The Serb won't be happy. "Get over here and into the trunk!"

The kid shuffles to the back of the car and shakes his head. "I don't think I can fit with all the merchandise."

Vito jabs the gun into the kid's gut. "Figure it out!"

Trays clatter on the ground, and the kid climbs into the empty trunk. "This, okay?"

"Lie down."

"Look, I don't really run the account. I'm only an intern. Sometimes they let me post on weekends. If you have a complaint, you can contact my manag—"

Vito fires three rounds into the kid's chest. Red stains turning Dodger Blue to a sickly purple. He slams the trunk closed.

Before leaving, Vito kneels at the pile of drawers, sorting through them.

"Huh, General Electric eighteen-by-twelve re-placement tray? This will finally get Angela off my back."

THE END

THE FAMILY BUSINESS

Evegeny slipped the Markov nine-millimeter into the shoulder holster and shrugged on his sports coat. As he crossed the room, Irina ignored him, not lifting her gaze from the television. He stepped onto the expansive balcony, and a stiff breeze off the Atlantic greeted him. Below, the white sands of Jupiter Island reflected the scorching heat of the midday sun. He cleared his throat. "Mikhail, I would speak with you."

Mikhail relaxed in a lounge chair, tapping away on his laptop. "Evegeny!" He beamed, shut the laptop and rose to hug his brother. "I will make us drinks."

Behind a well-stocked bar at the far end of the balcony, Mikhail mixed vodka with grapefruit juice into tall glasses filled with ice. He handed one to his brother. They turned to watch the breaking waves.

Evegeny frowned. "I am troubled by noises on the streets."

Mikhail sighed. "If you insist on a conversation about the family business, then *all* the family should be present."

Evegeny stifled a grunt. "You want to interrupt Irina's shows?" Their sister cared for nothing but the latest installment of *Real Housewives* and the fashions and shoes on display at the Aventura Mall. "This is a discussion between men. You've ceded West Palm to the Jamaicans and given away the cocaine trade to the Albanians. Albanians for God's sake. They're heathens!"

"I apologize for not consulting," Mikhail said. "But we're making more money than ever. It was time to abandon high-profile, risky endeavors. People get shot. The public makes demands. The police come down hard." His smile grew wide. "But with Medicare fraud, insurance fraud, everyone is paid: the doctors, the clinics, the patients. There are no bodies. No victims to complain. No one even suspects." He raised his glass high. "America, truly the land of opportunity."

Evegeny downed his drink and refilled it. His brother was always so sure of himself, but Father left Mikhail in charge, because he was the oldest, not the strongest. "No one doubts your inventive talents for making money. But it's dangerous to show weakness in the face of our rivals."

"Not weakness. Cleverness."

"They may not perceive it that way. And to our competitors, perception *is* reality."

Mikhail waved his hand dismissively. "Will you ever be satisfied? You have more money than you could ever hope to spend. What else do you want?"

Power. Respect. These are more important than wealth. That his brother couldn't understand proved Mikhail had been corrupted by the very country he was corrupting. "I want control."

Mikhail shook his head. "That is the wrong attitude. Forget the ego. Be smart."

Evegeny gulped his drink, set down the glass, and produced the pistol. "Now I am not smart?"

"Put that thing away."

"Do not tell me what to do." His face flushed. Why must Mikhail be so willful? "You will be permitted to continue peddling your insurance schemes, but I am running things."

"We can discuss this. But not at gunpoint."

The alcohol fueled Evegeny's rage. "No more talk." He raised the weapon.

"Be reasonable." Mikhail reached for the pistol.

"Enough!" Evegeny's finger twitched. The gun fired twice. Mikhail's shirt erupted in red and he dropped to the floor.

"No!" Evegeny fell to his knees and checked for a pulse. Nothing. He cradled Mikhail's head; empty blue eyes stared back. "See what you made me do, Brother? If only you weren't so stubborn."

He fought back tears and formulated a plan. He'd get the maid to clean up the mess and have Mikhail's driver dispose of the body. Evegeny would explain that the staff worked for him now. They would understand and do as they were told.

He booted up Mikhail's laptop. Password protected. His phone, too. No problem. He knew experts who dealt in such matters.

Taking on the Jamaicans would require plenty of men. He'd issue an ultimatum. Give them a we—

Gunshots erupted from behind. Evegeny's body exploded in pain. He gasped for air, but it wouldn't come. He collapsed on the floor. With great effort, he lifted his head and saw Irina staring down at him with contempt. Evegeny tried to speak. All that emerged from his throat was a low gurgle.

"Thank you, Dear Evegeny." His sister smiled cruelly. She kicked him in the ribs with the pointed toe of her zebra-patterned ankle boot and jabbed the stiletto heel into his chest. "I see we both had doubts about the direction of the family business." She pointed the gun at his head and fired.

THE END

PICTURE PERFECT

I read the evening edition of *The Press* with my feet propped on my desk, the only way I could stretch them in this peach crate I called an office. Willoughby, the hotel manager, had converted my old office into a bank of phone booths and relocated me next to the boiler room, deep in the basement of the Rudolph. I loosened my tie, angled the fan a bit, and flipped to the sporting page. The Cardinals were rolling up the National League like Russian tanks through the Germans at Kursk.

The exploits of the St. Louis Nine were interrupted by the ringing of my phone. "DeMille," I answered.

A whisper on the other end. Impossible to hear.

"You need to speak up."

"This is the front desk." A woman's voice. Still a whisper.

"To whom am I speaking?" I asked.

"It's Miss Adams."

Didn't recognize her name. Must be new. "What can I do for you, Miss Adams?"

"I'm concerned about a man who just checked in. Mr. Willoughby said if I had suspicions about a guest, I should contact the house detective."

Willoughby won't tolerate illicit activities in the Rudolph unless he's getting a cut. "Okay, Miss Adams, what's your concern?"

"The guest didn't want to sign the register, and he has no luggage," she said still in a whisper. "Frankly, he struck me as a real crumb."

Back in the day, rum runners were the hotel's biggest worry. I haven't run into any Nazi saboteurs, only the occasional cheating spouse. Most of my time was spent keeping the guests from pulling back the blackout curtains. "What's his name?" I grabbed a pencil.

"Leonard Wismer from Mays Landing. Dark-hair, thin and about five-six."

I jotted down the description and imagined Miss Adams' puffy lips, hovering close to the receiver, producing that soft, breathy whisper. "And what's his room number?"

"He's in 402."

That's one of the nicest suites in the hotel. Where you'll find the big wheels from the Main Line when they visit the shore. If this Wismer was up to something, it wasn't penny-ante. "Fine, I'll check up on him."

A chance to really stretch my legs. Later I could stop by the front desk and introduce myself in person to Miss Adams. I wanted to put a face and body to that sultry whisper. Redhead and medium height, I guessed. With a smattering of freckles.

***

I camped out on four in an alcove near the elevator. Three padded chairs, I sat in the middle one, and an end table. The hallway was muggy, and I mopped my brow. Couldn't open the window to let the breeze in because the curtain would flap and the hotel would get fined by the air raid warden.

My stake out of Wismer's room had lasted close to ninety minutes. No ladies of dubious virtue or slick-looking sharks had gone in or out. No one at all. The hands on the grandfather clock in the hallway read 9:55. Five minutes until Charlie, the assistant house detective, came on duty. Then off to the Crab Shack, grab some dinner, and find some female companionship. I was ready to make a pass at Laura, the new waitress from Philadelphia with the cutest brown peepers. Failing that, I'd drink until I didn't mind going home to Violet.

That's not fair. Violet's an okay gal and a fair cook. We have our good times, but it's against my nature to stick with only one lady. No matter what the Church says. We don't have kids, so no innocents are getting hurt. And I'm discreet. Most of the time. Well, I don't go out of my way to embarrass Violet.

I turned the page of the paper to find a headline blaring "Jersey Devil Spotted Near Hammonton – Youths Describe Encounter with Infernal Beast." Below was a crude drawing of a creature with a goat head and giant bat wings. A couple of teenagers hunting in the Pine Barrens claimed to have come across the beast. They shot at it to no effect and barely escaped with their lives.

As I continued to read about the monstrous encounter, the elevator doors slid open. I lowered the paper to catch a glimpse of a blonde stepping into the hall. Tall, almost five-ten in those the heels. She looked in my direction for a moment, her candy-apple red lips curled into a half-smile when we met eyes. Or eye. Under a black beret, she wore her hair Veronica Lake-style with a golden lock covering her right eye. Her left eye was as blue as a cloudless summer sky.

The Crab Shack could wait.

I studied Blondie's rocking hips and amazing gams as she glided down the hallway. Healthy and fit. No war-time rationing for her. She stopped at 402 and knocked. The door opened, and she stepped inside.

I folded my newspaper, laid it on the table, and stood. Floorboards creaked as I walked down the hallway, and I switched to tiptoeing. I pressed my ear against the door. A man and a woman talking. Impossible to make out the words.

The voices grew louder. Still couldn't understand what they were saying. Not sure it was English. Maybe German? Blondie did have an Aryan look to her.

A woman screamed. I grabbed the knob. Locked. A gunshot, something shattered, and a thud. With my pass key, I unlocked the door. To avoid being an easy target, I flattened myself against the wall and pushed the door open with my right foot. Another gunshot. I pulled out my revolver and peeked around the doorway.

A guy was face down on the floor. Cheap gray suit and the size of Wismer by the clerk's description. Shards of a shattered vase laid next to him. Blondie stood over him with a pistol in her hand.

I pointed my revolver at her. "Drop it and reach for the sky, Sister."

She gave me that same mysterious half-smile from the hallway and the gun clattered to the floor.

Keeping her covered, I knelt by the body. Blood stained the carpet. Willoughby would be livid at the cleaning bill. Checked for a pulse. Nothing.

Before I even asked, she said, "It was self-defense."

The vase broke after the first gunshot. Maybe he had it in his hands, ready to strike, she shot him, and *then* it fell to the floor. More likely she was lying, but no need to let on that I suspected.

I picked up her pistol, a .38 revolver, and shoved both guns in my pocket. The scent of lilacs cut through the odor of gunpowder. But more than her perfume, I smelled money. Her emerald green dress didn't come off the rack and those reptile-skin pumps must cost more than I make in a month. A rich and beautiful dame in trouble? The possibilities were endless.

I trotted out my best reassuring smile. "I'd Edward DeMille, the house detective. Why don't we sit down and you can tell me what happened?"

She nodded, and we took seats at opposite ends of an olive, thee-person davenport.

"I'm Mrs. Herbert Floyd."

Her words were calm and cool. That's not an indictment. People react differently to death. Even if they're the one responsible. I should know. And I was right about the money. Herbert Floyd owned banks, railroads, factories, and most of the state legislature.

I glanced at the body. "And who is the deceased gentleman on the floor, Mrs. Floyd?"

"Please call me, Nancy." She frowned. "His name is Leonard Wismer. But he's no gentleman."

"No?" I raised an eyebrow.

She shook her head. "He has... photos... of me." Tears welled up in that big blue eye. First sign of any emotion.

I offered her my handkerchief. On her forefinger a gold class ring from Atlantic City High, just like Violet's. Local girl does well, or rather marries well. "I'm guessing they're not picture portraits?"

"No." She dabbed at her tears. "A scandal would ruin my husband, us."

"Wismer was blackmailing you?"

She nodded, and the waterworks flowed.

"How much?"

"Five thousand dollars. Each of the past three months."

A let out a low whistle. "And you were to pay him again tonight?"

"Yes, but I couldn't raise the money."

"Five thousand is a lot of dough for most people, but not your husband."

She shook her head. "He doesn't know. He can't know. Herbert has me on an allowance. I pawned my jewelry to make the earlier payments."

"And you told Wismer this when you met tonight?"

"Yes." She nodded. "When I told him, I didn't have the money, he became furious. Said he'd tell

Herbert. That's when I pulled the gun. I just wanted the photos. I wasn't going to shoot him. I never used a gun before. But he grabbed the vase and threw it at me. I don't even remember shooting him." She edged closer.

The vase wasn't thrown. More evidence she was jerking me around? Or was she in shock and not remembering clearly? If she was all fired up, could she pull the trigger on the revolver twice and not realize it? But she didn't shoot twice in succession. The body hit the floor, then the second shot came, which suggested deliberate action.

"You don't believe me?" she said reading the doubt on my face. The tears stopped. Did she realize they weren't having the desired effect?

I shrugged. "Doesn't matter what I believe. That's a matter for the police and the courts."

"The police? Do they have to be involved?" She leaned forward and clutched my arm.

"There's a dead man on the floor. And you dusted him."

She stared at me with that solitary blue eye. "If the police get hold of the photos, it's a sure bet the papers will have them next. I can't let that happen." Her hand slid across my jacket and fingered my lapel.

With the Rudolphs's thick walls, it was likely no one else heard the gunshots. Gave me time to come up with a plan for both the money *and* the dame. "Do we know if he brought the photos with him?"

She nodded. "Tonight was supposed to be the last payoff. He was going to turn them over to me."

I gently removed her hand, stood, and made my way to the body. I knelt next to Wismer, hefted him over, and smiled. "He told you his name was Leonard Wismer?"

Nancy looked puzzled. "Why?"

"Because his real name is Vinnie Octaroro. He's a blackmailer all right." And more. A few years ago, Octaroro took a couple of potshots at me while I was running protection on the docks. I paid him back with a busted nose and a broken collarbone for his trouble. Mrs. Floyd had done me and the world a favor.

"What does that mean?" Her voice filled with concern.

I sighed. "Probably nothing. Makes sense that Octaroro would use an alias." I searched his pockets. In his pants I found a wallet with twenty-four dollars and close to fifty meat and gas stamps, ripped from their ration books. Vinnie had expanded from blackmail to the black market. In his inner coat pocket was a sealed envelope with what felt like thick papers inside. Could be the photographs.

Nancy knelt next to me, her arm brushing mine. The air thick with her lilac perfume, like I was in the middle of a flower garden in June. She reached for the envelope, her hand touching mine. Her faint breath on my cheek. "I need those." Her voice a whisper that seemed oddly familiar.

I swallowed hard and kept my grip on the envelope. Those photos were my meal ticket out of the basement and beyond. Across his business empire, Herbert Floyd must have need of a problem solver. I scrambled back to the couch. "Octaroro didn't have a gun. That could be a problem."

She sat next to me. "I told you. He came at me with a vase."

"You said he threw it at you. But it's next to his body. Like he was holding it when he was shot."

"What are you saying, Eddie?"

Now I'm Eddie? "I'm saying, I can help you, but only if you play it straight with me." I fingered the envelope. "These photos provide a powerful motive. And there's no doubt you shot him."

She leaned closer. "And you can help me with that?"

Help her with a story? Or disposing of Vinnie? Could I get the body out of the hotel without being seen? Then dump him in the ocean? What was my incentive for risking multiple felonies? Just what was Mrs. Floyd offering?

Nancy pressed her leg against mine. "Would money help?"

"Money *always* helps. But I thought you were tapped out? The allowance and all that."

"I could get more. But it would take time." She slid her arms around me. "Or we could work out a trade." She pulled me close and kissed my cheek. She nibbled on my ear. "Help me, Eddie."

I kissed her, long and hard. Didn't stop until I needed more air. I broke the embrace.

She leaned back, her lips curled in to that half-smile, and my decision was made. I would help her *and* myself.

"Okay," I said still gasping for air. "I need to think of a plan." At that moment wracking my brain required more effort than usual. "We need to know if these are the photographs. If not, I'll rummage around Octaroro's place." I paused. "Need to search it anyway, in case he made copies." I didn't need *another* blackmailer complicating things.

With my penknife, I slit open the envelope. Twenty-or-so photographs tumbled to the floor. I reached to grab them. There's not much that shocks me, but these photos were indecent, prurient, obscene.

And not of Nancy.

They were of Violet.

The doorknob jiggled.

Nancy screamed. She tossed her beret on the floor, tousled her hair, and ripped the collar of her dress.

The door flew off its hinges and crashed to the floor. Lt. Scanlon and a couple of his blue-coated gorillas entered, guns in hand.

"Thank God, you're here," said Nancy. She raced across the room, hiding behind an officer and clutching his arm. "He killed that man and tried to attack me." The tears flowed again like she turned on a faucet.

And now it made sense. Starting with the now familiar whispers of the *desk clerk.*

Scanlon grinned at me with crooked teeth. "Well, well. What have we got here?" He looked at Octaroro's body. "Well-known underworld figure shot dead. Up to your old tricks, Eddie?"

My mouth went dry. No way some hotel guest heard the shots, called the police, and they got here this quick. Someone tipped Scanlon in advance, or he's in on it. Add in the photos of Violet and my history with Octaroro and the noose was tightening around my neck.

In the hallway, the gongs of the grandfather clock began. Ten o'clock. Violet and her classmate Nancy hung a picture-perfect frame on me and it only took five minutes.

THE END

OUTSOURCING

2021 Derringer Award Finalist

Johnny Maggio's wife was having an affair. But a divorce was out of the question, as the Church frowned on such measures. Instead, Johnny chose to have this lothario rubbed out. The Church also felt rather strongly about murder, but this was a matter of pride.

The Romeo in question was Vinnie "Two Cats" Castiglione, a small-time hood with a gambling problem. Johnny wasn't inclined to wade through all the dive bars, meth dens, and floating crap games on the West Side to hunt down some third-rater. Johnny gave the job to his lieutenant, Tommy Octaroro, plus fifty grand for Tommy's trouble.

***

Through the wages of sin, Tommy Octaroro had achieved a prosperous life including a seven-bedroom, five-and-a-half bath, McMansion on the North Shore, a forty-eight-foot ketch moored at the yacht club, and a high-rise condo in South Beach. Tommy wasn't willing to lose all that to eradicate some low-life who crossed the boss. Too many risks: cops, witnesses, a retaliatory lucky shot by Vinnie.

At Sunday family dinner, his sister Julie again whined to Tommy about advancement for her son Donny. The boy was good with numbers, but seemed to lack a certain malevolence necessary to succeed in their world. This was the kid's lucky day; Tommy promised his nephew twenty-five thou and the opportunity to make his bones.

***

Donny Stillwell liked the idea of being a made man and all that came with it: the respect, the money, the ladies. Especially the ladies. But he didn't want to have to kill someone. In almost all the fights he'd been in, going back to grade school, he came out the loser. And he was deathly afraid of firearms. But he was more terrified of his Uncle Tommy, so he accepted the assignment.

But that didn't mean Donny had to be the one who pulled the trigger. He figured to subcontract the work, enjoying all the benefits of the transaction, while avoiding any danger of physical injury.

He reviewed his list of underworld associates. The Dominicans were too hot-headed. The Nigerians too untrustworthy. In the end, he selected a pair of Moldovan brothers he worked with exporting stolen luxury sedans to Eastern Europe, and offered them ten G's, to take care of Vinnie.

***

The Ceban brothers, Timur and Vadin, undertook the commission because they didn't wish to anger Donny and lose the franchise running misappropriated Mercedes to Romania. But the brothers were smugglers, not killers. Neither owned a gun. To perform the deed, they hired a recently arrived Armenian immigrant. The man had served in his nation's special forces and was reputed to have assassinated of a rogue Azerbaijani General.

***

Sak Arakelian was eager to build a reputation in his newly adopted country and took the Moldovan's deal. But he was still unfamiliar with America and didn't want to make a fatal error with his first murder-for-hire. So he posted an ad on Craigslist under "Services Wanted."

***

Inside the local bar, a man approached Arakelian, but did not sit. "You posted the ad?"

"Are you a cop?" Arakelian asked.

"Do I look like a cop?"

The man didn't look like an American cop, at least not the ones Sak had seen on television. His hair wasn't perfectly coiffed. His teeth weren't gleaming white. He didn't wear the latest expensive fashions. "No, you don't."

"How much?" asked the man who didn't look like a cop.

"Two thousand," Arakelian said, keeping three for himself.

The man nodded. "Who's the target?"

"A hoodlum named Vinnie Castiglione. Do you know him?"

The man stiffened and blinked rapidly.

"Is that a problem?" Arakelian asked.

The man relaxed and shook his head. "I know where to find him."

"Half now. Half when job is done." Arakelian slid an envelope across the table.

The man who didn't look like a cop took the envelope, stuffed it in his jacket pocket, and departed.

***

In his car the man counted the money, punched the address of an Atlantic City casino into his GPS, and started the engine. From the backseat came a pair of high-pitched meows. He turned and reached with both hands to scratch their ears.

"Luck's running our way, Girls. Get ready for a little road trip."

THE END

THE PROS AND CONS OF TIME TRAVEL

"You have a time machine?" Arthur Wilbur looked more CPA than angel investor: five-six, wire-rimmed glasses, bowtie, tweed jacket.

Dina, arms crossed over her gray M.I.T. sweatshirt, said, "I can't discuss anything until you sign the NDA."

Without reading, Wilbur scribbled his signature and handed the sheet to Dina's partner, Jarrod.

Jarrod scanned the document. "Excellent." He smiled, a gap between his front teeth, and stuck the paper in a filing cabinet. "We *do* have a time machine. Please follow us."

The pair led Wilbur from the cramped office down an unpainted hallway.

"No security?" Wilbur craned his neck, looking for cameras.

Dina shook her head. "We put all our capital into the device."

The three exited the hallway into an open loft, fifty-feet square.

"And here it is." Dina stood next to a metal platform, caressing it like a game show model.

In the center of a metal platform stood a glass cylinder, meter and a half tall, sixty centimeters in diameter. Dull white floor. Open door in its side. Colorful wires: purple, green, orange, snaked from its wide base, three times the width of the chamber. A pair of hoses connected to the conical brass top.

On the left: a panel as tall as Wilbur filled with dials, switches, readouts, and blinking lights. To the right: four folding tables covered with computer towers and monitors.

"That's our research." Dina pointed to half-a-dozen bookshelves filled with journals.

Wilbur grabbed a notebook. Jarrod swallowed hard, wondering if this egg could make sense of the numbers, Greek letters, and sketches.

Wilbur re-shelved the book. "How about a demonstration?"

"Of course." Dina handed him a sheet of paper and envelope. "Write something only you would know."

Wilbur scrawled the name of the first girl he kissed. Dina took the envelope, laid it in the center of the cylinder, and locked the chamber.

The green LED readout atop the panel flashed: 98

Dina sat at one of the tables, typing, glancing between a pair of forty-inch monitors.

"We're going to send it forward a little over a minute and a half." Jarrod stood at the control panel, flipping switches.

Fog, sublimating carbon dioxide from the dry ice hidden in the platform, filled the chamber.

"What's that?" Wilbur asked.

"Field density is increasing," Dina said. "It's a side effect of the charged particles."

Once the envelope was obscured, Jarrod turned a dial. The floor of the chamber lowered one inch. An identical floor rotated into place. When the fog cleared, the envelope appeared to have vanished.

Wilbur raised an eyebrow.

Green numbers counted down: 45...44...43...

At twenty seconds, the fog returned. Jarrod spun the dial in the opposite direction. The "process" that sent the envelope into the future reversed. When the air cleared, the envelope lay in its original position. Dina retrieved it from the chamber.

Wilbur tore open the envelope, and recognized his handwriting. "Ninety-eight seconds? Can you go further?"

"The power requirements increase with the cube of the distance traveled in time," Jarrod said. "Same goes for mass."

Dina said, "We need more power, which means more money. Last month our electric bill was mid-five figures."

Wilbur scratched his chin. "You can send things forward. What about back?"

"We're close." Dina held her thumb and finger a millimeter apart. "But we need capital."

"How much?" Wilbur asked.

Dina and Jarrod looked at each other. Sick of peanut grifts, their plan was to ask for five million. But this mark seemed eager to bite.

"Ten million." Dina watched Wilbur's reaction.

The investor didn't blink.

Dina's heart pounded. She never felt as alive as when bumping a rube. "That's to move heavier objects forward. Fifteen million to go back."

Wilbur glanced at the chamber, panel, computers. "I'll need to speak with my associates. They may wish to see with their own eyes."

Jarrod frowned. Each demonstration increased the risk of being found out. "We thought you were the decision maker."

"Perhaps I *can* decide," Wilbur said. "Tell me how this works."

"Do you have a PhD in theoretical physics?" Jarrod asked.

"Or a basic understanding of quantum teleportation?" Dina said.

"Fair enough." Wilbur shrugged.

Jarrod sensed he should apply pressure. "We have a potential investor visiting later this week. She represents foreign interests. Dina and I would like backing from Americans, but we'll do what's necessary."

"Anyone else with knowledge of this project?"

"Just us," Jarrod said. "None of our colleagues, no one at the university, have a hint."

"Secrecy is a must," Dina added. "We worry about other scientists, but also the government. If the Feds knew what we were up to, they'd swoop in with some bullshit excuse about National Security, shut us down, and steal our research."

Wilbur smiled at that. "I'm pleased with your discretion." He reached under his jacket, pulling the silenced semi-automatic from his shoulder holster.

Jarrod raised his hands, confusion on his face. Wilbur fired three times into his chest. Jarrod's shirt erupted in a sea of red.

Dina screamed, turned, and made it two steps before bullets pierced her lungs and kidneys. She fell to the ground, gurgling sounds coming from her mouth.

Always thorough, Wilbur added a headshot to each.

He returned to his car, retrieving a tire iron and two cans of gasoline. With one swing, the time chamber shattered into a thousand shards. He gathered up the notebooks of research, doused them with gas, and lit a match. Flames engulfed the room.

By the time Wilbur drove away, smoke billowed from the windows of the building.

He phoned his superior. "I finished with the pair in Cambridge. They achieved minor forward displacement. Nothing backward. No chance they could have disrupted our operations."

"Any idea what method they were using?"

"You want answers to questions like that? Send a tech, not an enforcer."

"Touché." His boss sighed. "You free for lunch?"

Wilbur glanced at the chronoscope on his wrist. "Yeah, give me twenty subjective minutes. How does *Prunier* in Paris 1925 sound?"

THE END

THE SOLAR PUNKS

Holst's *Mars, Bringer of War* blared from the sky above McLaughlin Ford.

Danny, the lot attendant, raised his hand to shield his eyes. A swarm of a dozen quadcopters descended out of the sun—like World War II enemy fighters—targeting the dealership's recently arrived inventory.

"Get the jammer!" Danny raced to the entrance of the service department, pulled open the door, and rushed inside.

The drones' music ended, replaced with an AI-generated female voice with a hint of an up-country Carolina accent. "Give up your carbon dioxide-spewing vehicles. Small actions, big impact. Let's go green!"

The quadcopters dive-bombed a row of new model year F-250s. Upon impact, the payload of plastic spheres shattered, covering the freshly waxed trucks with orange slime.

Danny emerged from the building, in his hand the military-grade, green-camo jammer, the size of a George R. R. Martin hardcover. He flicked on the power and aimed the device at the departing attackers.

Eleven of the drones appeared out of range. They flew up and across the highway, disappearing from view. But the last circled like a drunken bumble bee, colliding with the giant American flag flying from the roof. The copter plummeted to the ground, smashing to pieces on the pavement in front of the parts department.

Emblazoned on the largest surviving shard was the image of an anthropomorphic sun sporting a mohawk haircut.

The logo of The Solar Punks.

***

Across the city, The Solar Punks' war on environmental degradation continued.

They hacked a group of video billboards, replacing the ads for airline tips to tropical destinations and developments of five-bedroom McMansions with a video of a man in a balaclava, while the list of the Solar Punks demands played on a scroll. When the billboard company regained control, a power surge fried the circuitry, leaving the high-def video screens permanently dark.

At a wooded site being cleared for an outdoor mixed-use lifestyle center, they reprogrammed the firmware of all the construction equipment, ensuring that the engines would never start again.

And in a nod to old-school vandalism, The Solar Punks dumped sand in the gas tanks and oil crankcases of the local electric utility's fleet of service vans, trucks, and cherry-pickers.

***

The Mayor cringed as he watched the security camera footage of the individual wearing a Guy Fawkes mask, armed with a shotgun, blasting away at an electrical substation.

"Do we have any leads?" he asked the Chief of Police.

The Chief shook her head. "The Solar Punks aren't listed in any terrorist database. Homeland Security has nothing on them." She sighed. "We ran the serial number of the drone recovered from the Ford dealership. Built in Estonia. Sold to a shell company in Dubai. No trail after that. These guys, whoever they are, are good."

"Maybe I need a better Chief?"

The Chief pursed her lips. "If you really think that will make a difference, you can have my resignation."

"Hell, no." The Mayor gave a weak smile. "I'm just frustrated."

"Me, too. And the whole department. I had my guys set up a sting. They organized a monster truck rally. A target so tempting the Solar Punks shouldn't be able to resist." She pounded her fist in her hand. "But nothing happened. Almost like they knew it was a setup."

"The most annoying part of all of this is: The Punks and I want the same thing," the Mayor said. "A cleaner, greener world. But they're going about this all wrong..."

***

Citizens packed the next City Council meeting.

"This is the third attack," Charlie McLaughlin said into the microphone. "And that wasn't paint they dumped on my trucks. It was some kind of plant-based solvent. Ate through the metal. Destroyed nineteen trucks. Had to sell them for scrap. Over a million dollars of inventory lost. And insurance won't cover it. Said damage due to 'civil unrest' is excluded."

The Mayor said, "That's unfortunate, Mr. McLaughlin, and the entire council and I sympathize with you. But this portion of the meeting is open for comments about agenda items. Comments of a general nature will be welcomed later."

"This *is* about the agenda." McLaughlin pointed his finger at the Mayor. "Your Little Green Deal is exactly what these Solar Punks are demanding. The city is capitulating to terrorists and fanatics."

Citizens stood, waved placards, and chanted, "Don't give in to punks!"

"We're not giving into terrorism." The Mayor struggled not to roll his eyes. "And it's not *My* Little Green Deal. It's everyone's. This is a chance to do our part. If every county, city, and town adopted these reforms, the planet would heal."

McLaughlin said, "Maybe focus on jobs, building our standard of living, and locking up these criminals."

The Mayor said, "The Little Green Deal is about more than saving the environment. These proposals and reforms mean investments in education, employment, and communities. The plan will pay for itself, *and* we get a more sustainable world."

***

The heated remarks from outraged citizens, combined with the pressure from their largest campaign contributors persuaded two councilwomen to change their votes. Every item on the Mayor's agenda went down to defeat: the wind farm, rooftop community gardens, installation of EV fast-charging stations at City Hall, the gas stove replacement rebate, and the rest. All by a four-to-three vote.

The Little Green Deal was dead.

***

Miles outside the city, The Consultant drove down a dirt driveway. He pulled up outside a dilapidated farmhouse and honked the horn.

A man in a faded army jacket emerged from the house and approached the car.

The Consultant handed the man an envelope full of cash. "There's a bonus in there for you and your team."

The man peeked in the envelope and smiled. "What's next?"

"New Jersey." The Consultant offered a manilla folder. "Light-rail planned from Camden to Glassboro. The vote is next month."

The man nodded. "Not a problem."

THE END

THE LAST CASE

Morris stood at the gravestone next to the woman in black.

Lori Inverso
1974-2018
Beloved Daughter and Sister

"Guess 'Beloved Wife' was out of the question," he muttered.

***

"And the last time you saw your wife?" asked Detective Morris.

Paul Inverso sighed. "Friday, when she left for work. We've been over this a dozen times."

"And this was at was seven-thirty?"

"Yes, seven-thirty in the morning," said Paul. His irritation was obvious.

The detective jotted in his notebook. "I understand you're upset, Mr. Inverso. We're just making sure we didn't miss anything. Any troubles in your marriage?"

"Nope, everything is fine."

An officer descended the steps carrying a PC tower.

"Hey, I gave you Lori's laptop," said Paul. "The computer is mine."

"She doesn't use it?" asked Morris.

Paul frowned. "I guess she does sometimes."

"Any objections to having our techs look at it?"

"No, I just want you to find her."

The detective nodded. With almost twenty-five years on the force, Morris could tell the difference between the truth and a lie.

***

"You claimed everything is fine with your marriage," said Morris.

"It is," said Inverso.

"Do you know a woman Jane Catlin?"

"Sure, she's a friend of Lori's. Lives a couple of blocks over."

"How would you characterize your relationship with Ms. Catlin?"

"We're friendly, neighborly. Like I said, she's more of Lori's friend."

Morris flipped through his notes. "I spoke with Ms. Catlin this morning. According to her characterization, you're more the friend than Lori."

Paul remained silent.

"Are you sure you don't want to rethink your last answer?"

"Okay, I'm sleeping with Jane."

Morris sighed. "It's never a good idea to lie to the police. But it's especially unhelpful when we're trying to find your wife."

"Lori has no idea. Jane means nothing to me. Just a harmless flirtation."

"Ms. Catlin seems to think it's more than a flirtation. Says you were going to leave Lori."

"Jane's imagining something that isn't there. I would never leave Lori."

***

"The techs found something unusual on your computer," said Morris.

"Unusual how?" asked Paul.

"Internet searches for 'How to dispose of a body?' and 'Ways to speed up decomposition.'"

"I don't know anything about that."

***

"Any recent changes in Lori's behavior?" asked Morris.

"She did get a phone call a earlier this month," said Paul. "It seemed to upset her, but she wouldn't tell me what it was about."

"What about her routine?"

"The past couple of weeks, she pulled a few double-shifts at work." Paul paused. "Or at least she said she was working. I was able to hide my affair from her. Maybe she hid one from me. You should ask her co-workers at the donut shop."

"We did. If she were having an affair, no one noticed."

***

We found your wife's car submerged in a lake in the Pine Barrens," said Morris.

"And Lori?" asked Paul.

"No body. No personal belongings. But we did find your cell phone in the car. Any idea how it got there?"

"It disappeared around the same time Lori did. I had to go to Verizon and get a replacement. She must have grabbed mine by mistake. She's done it before."

"If she grabbed yours by mistake, then her phone should be in the house. Have you seen it?"

Paul shook his head.

***

"We found some odd charges on your credit card," said Morris.

"What do you mean *odd?*" asked Paul.

"Morturary.com. Apothecaries 'R' Us."

"I've never even heard of them."

"We pulled the orders. They shipped eight pounds of sodium hydroxide. That's lye. And a cadaver bag."

"This has to be a set up."

"Really, Mr. Inverso? Who would set you up *and* have access to your credit card?"

"How about Jane? Maybe she finally realized I wouldn't leave Lori."

"That's not what she claims."

"She's lying. Where was she when Lori disappeared?"

"We checked. She was at the NJEA Convention in Atlantic City from Thursday to Sunday. Twenty witnesses place her there."

"Maybe, she has an accomplice."

"Like a lover?"

***

"Paul Inverso, you are under arrest for the murder of your wife, Lori Inverso," said Morris.

"I didn't do it!" said Paul.

***

Inverso Sentenced to Life in Prison read the headline. The detective put down the paper. Now he could retire.

***

"Guess 'Beloved Wife' was out of the question," Morris muttered.

The woman in black chuckled. She wrapped her arms around him and pulled close. "What now?" asked Lori.

"We start our new life together," said the ex-detective.

THE END

THOUGHT EXPERIMENT

The trolley races down the hill. The operator is unconscious, slumped over the controls. At the bottom of the hill a group of five cheerleaders gather on the tracks.

Alan shouts at the cheerleaders. They don't hear him. He waves his arms. They're taking a selfie.

He spies a switch next to the tracks. He sprints, grabs and yanks. It will not budge. He pulls again. Nothing. The trolley is gathering speed. Alan plants his feet against the base and leans his body away, using all his weight. The metal creaks. Bit by bit, the lever moves. The trolley is almost there.

Alan strains. Sweat drips down his face.

Click!

The track has shifted. The trolley rattles past and heads onto a siding. The cheerleaders are saved.

But a man is standing on this other track, his back to the trolley. Pedestrians scream, but he's wearing ear buds. People watch in horror as the trolley drags his body beneath its wheels.

***

Ten minutes later, the ambulance arrives. The paramedics can do nothing. Death was instantaneous.

The deceased's name is Bill Doyle. Thirty-two. Has a pretty blonde wife named Dana. No kids. Lifelong resident of the city. Works downtown in the 1st National Trust Building.

***

The debate rages over the ethics of Alan's actions.

The Unitarian minister argues pulling the lever was the right thing to do. "Yes, it's a tragedy about Bill," she says. "But if Alan didn't act, all those girls would have died. That's much worse. Five lives trump one."

The Chair of the Philosophy Department at the local university disagrees. "Head down this utilitarian path paved with good intentions and you'll save five people in need of transplants, by killing one healthy patient to harvest his organs."

***

At home one evening Alan's phone chirps. He checks his message and shouts to his wife, Carol. "I'm going to the bar!" Before she answers, he's out the door.

He walks past the bar and turns down an alley. In the dim light a figure approaches. It's Dana, Bill's widow.

Alan reaches into his coat pocket and retrieves a pistol.

Her eyes grow wide. "Put that thing away," she says.

He looks at the gun and shoves it back in his pocket. "Are you getting cold feet?"

"Of course not." She wraps her arms around him and presses her lips to his.

He kisses her back enthusiastically. "If you don't want the gun, then what's the plan?"

She glances at her watch. "Right about now a package is being delivered to your wife."

"What's in the package?"

Dana smiles. "A radioactive isotope, a Geiger counter, and a vial of poison gas."

***

"I was at the bar. I had nothing to do with my wife's death." Alan is sitting in a metal chair, handcuffed to a table in a dull gray interrogation room.

"Nope," says the detective. He picks up a folder. "The M.E.'s report says your wife was in a state of quantum superposition. Then you come home and wham!" He slams his open palm on the table. "You collapsed the wave function and she's dead."

"You can't prove anything," says Alan.

The detective reads from the report. "Time of death is 11:05pm. The exact moment you arrived home."

"That's crazy."

"Your girlfriend's talking with my partner right now." He sneers. "Whichever one of you talks first gets to live."

Alan does the math. If he says nothing, they have him on the gun charge. Good for a year, maybe eighteen months. If Dana or he betrays the other, one will go free while the other heads to the gallows. If they both confess, they'll live, but each face a long prison sentence.

They'd both be better off if neither confesses. But he can't be sure what she'll do. He has to act in his own self-interest. Cold hard logic, trumps love. *Sorry, Dana.*

"Okay, I'll t—"

The detective's partner walks in the room. "Dana just flipped. And that's not all. Seems they had a plot to kill her husband as well. The trolley was a fortunate coincidence."

The first detective laughs and runs his finger across this throat.

***

With dozens of eyewitnesses to Alan's actions and the testimony of Dana, the prosecution has a slam-dunk case. In less than an hour the jury returns verdicts of guilty on two counts of Murder in the First Degree.

"I can't sentence you to hang more than once, but I will add this stipulation," says the judge. "It is the order of this court that Alan Albertson be hung at dawn on a day next week to be determined by the

Department of Corrections. But the condemned is not to know when his life will end until the morning of the appointed day."

The courtroom gasps. The judge bangs his gavel. No one notices the smile on Alan's face.

****

The jailer brings Alan his dinner. "You seem awfully cheery for a man facing death."

"That's the thing. The judge fouled it all up. I'm safe as the gold in Fort Knox."

"How so?"

"The judge said I have to be hung next week, Monday-to-Sunday, but I am not allowed to know what day it will happen."

"Right."

"Well, I can't be hung Sunday. When I wake up Saturday morning and they don't hang me, I know it's got to be Sunday. But I'm not allowed to know. So, Sunday is out."

"Just hang you on Saturday," says the jailer.

Alan shakes his head. "Since Sunday is out, when I wake up Friday morning and they don't hang me, it will have to be Saturday. But if I know it's Saturday, then that's out too."

The jailer lets out a low whistle.

"By the same process Friday is out, then Thursday, and so on." Alan laughs. "That old judge was too clever by half. I'm certain to outlive him."

****

Wednesday morning Alan is eating breakfast in his cell. He's completely surprised when the jailers arrive to take him to the gallows.

THE END

TOUGH GAME

Dubler positioned himself five feet from the bag, pounded his fist into his glove, and leaned forward on the balls of his feet.

Nakamura's pitch was inside. Murphy turned on it, hammering the ball down the third base line. Dubler stuck out his glove. He couldn't field it, but managed to knock it down. After a mad scramble, and with no time to look back the runner at second, he launched his throw to first base. The ball sailed wildly over Arroyo's outstretched glove into the stands.

Dubler, hands on his hips, kicked at the dirt, and stared at the ground.

"Batter to second base, and the runner on second will score, giving the Monarchs the lead," the radio announcer told his listeners. "Dubler's having a tough game. Struck out twice and that's his third error in as many innings."

A series of boos filled the air as the Dragons' fans registered their displeasure with Dubler's performance. But in the front row, a man in a gray suit and a fedora smiled.

***

"One out in the bottom of the ninth and the Dragons have men on first and second," the announcer said. "Finally, a chance for Dubler to redeem himself. He's oh for four on the day with three strike outs. Last time up in the seventh, he tapped a weak grounder to second."

Dubler walked toward the batter's box, his face etched with grim determination. The fans greeted him with a Bronx cheer.

The first pitch was a fastball high and inside, sending Dubler to the ground.

"Ball one!" called the umpire.

Dubler stared down the pitcher and gritted his teeth.

The second pitch broke early and in the dirt. Dubler, appearing to be badly fooled, swung and missed. The spin on the ball sent it bouncing away from the catcher all the way to the wall. The runners advanced to second and third. With first base open, the opposing manager called for an intentional walk, taking the bat out of Dubler's hands.

He walked sullenly to first base, and felt the pit in his stomach grow. Before he had time to formulate a plan, Gorman crushed the first pitch over the left field wall for a game-winning grand slam.

Twenty thousand happy Dragons' fans celebrated deliriously. The man in the fedora didn't.

***

Dubler sat in front of his locker, his head drooping.

"Don't be low. We won!" Arroyo slapped him on the shoulder. "You had a tough game, amigo. But that's okay, we're here to pick each other up."

Dubler looked up and managed a weak smile.

"Tough game, Dubler." Carolyn Rodgers, the blond reporter from the cable station thrust a microphone in his face. "What happened out there?"

Dubler slapped the microphone away. "Why don't you talk to Gorman? He's the hero."

"Hey guys!" shouted Simmons. "Who's up for a little fun tonight at Engine Forty-Nine? First round's on me."

The clubhouse roared with approval.

"How about you, Dubler?"

Dubler shook his head. "You guys go on without me. I think I might be coming down with the flu."

"What's that?" Scott Blackbell, the Dragon's manager, pointed a bony finger at Dubler. "Next time, you're feeling sick, let me know. Don't pull that ironman crap on me."

"Sure thing, Skipper."

***

Dubler avoided the remaining reporters, showered, and picked at the food from the post-game spread.

When there was no one left in the clubhouse, he grabbed his bag and walked to his truck.

In the gloom he saw a small figure lingering near his F-250. Was it some kid waiting for an autograph? Security was supposed to keep them away. As he got closer to the truck, he recognized Louie in his trademark fedora. Dubler swallowed hard.

"Hey there, Mr. Baseball," Louie said. "You really let me down today."

Dubler shook his head. "Did you see the game? I did my worst without being obvious about it."

"Oh. I saw. But this is the third time you've been a disappointment. My friends are out a lot of money, and they're not happy."

"Look, I'll do better, or rather worse, tomorrow," Dubler said. "It was a really tough game."

"Things are going to get a whole lot tougher." Louie pulled out a stainless-steel semi-auto pistol and fired twice into Dubler's chest.

Dubler fell to the ground, his eyes filled with disbelief.

"You play baseball, you know the rules. Today was your third strike," Louie said. "And now you're out."

THE END

FAST TIMES AT SPIRO AGNEW HIGH

7:38 a.m.

I'm about to step off the bus and I make like a statue. Frank Samson is standing on the curb, between me and the school, dressed like an undertaker's apprentice: white shirt, dark tie, black slacks.

"Wimmer, you're blocking traffic," a voice says from behind.

Samson flashes a rat-faced smile and punches a fist into his open hand.

"Move!" Someone shoves me.

I tumble to the pavement. Frank takes two steps toward me, then I'm up and running for my life. I head left toward the staff parking lot. Two hundred yards and twenty-five seconds later, I look over my shoulder. No Samson.

I'm sucking wind as I duck between a gray SUV and a fire engine red Mustang. If I can slip inside the school, maybe use the west entrance, I can avoid him till at least lunch. By then I'll come up with a plan. I fig—

"Going somewhere, Wimmer?" Powerful hands grab me, slamming me onto the hood of the Mustang. I'm face-to-face with Chris Unrath. His breath smells of Frosted Flakes and orange juice. A bulging red vein slices through his blond crew cut. Muscles swell under his too tight Orioles t-shirt. Rumor is he was kicked off the wrestling team after testing positive for steroids.

"Yeah, headed to first-period history. Got a quiz on the Hapsburg Empire. Do you have any insights into their demise?"

"Is that supposed to be funny?" Unrath lifts me off the hood and my shirt begins to rip.

"I never joke about European dynasties."

He tosses me to the ground. The sole of his muddy work boot hovers above my head. Before he can stomp me into next week, shined black shoes step next to my face.

"Hold off, Chris."

Samson! No wonder he didn't chase after me. But who wears designer Italian wingtips to school? This isn't Georgetown Prep.

I tilt my head and glance up. Samson's eyes are black as coal, black as his heart. I struggle to my feet.

"Wimmer, Wimmer, Wimmer. You know better than to run." Samson consults his phone. "You owe me two hundred dollars."

Last Friday we were manhandling VoTech. My big chance to get even. Then our All-County place kicker shanks a chip shot field goal so far to the right it might have landed in the bay. First time he's missed all season. Didn't matter. We were up by three touchdowns. As for the spread...

"It can't be that much." I shake my head.

Samson laughs like a supervillain explaining his plans to the helpless hero. "I love the power of compound interest. It's a Goddamn miracle."

"Give me one more chance."

"Nope. Your credit has been cut off." He reaches into my jacket, pulls out my wallet, and rifles it.

"Give it!" I make a fist, but Unrath grabs my arm and twists it behind my back. He slips me into a half nelson. If he pushes my head any farther forward, it might pop off.

"Twelve dollars and a gift card to Buffalo Wild Wings?" Samson stuffs them into his pocket. He holds up a photo and squints. "Who's the blonde? Definitely too nice for you."

"She's from Canada. You wouldn't know her."

Unrath releases my head and delivers a shot to my stomach. Good thing I skipped breakfast, or it'd be all over the parking lot.

Samson rips the photo in halves, quarters, eighths, and tosses the confetti at me. "Here's the deal, Wimmer. Kickoff against Mandel is at six tonight. You get me my money by game time, or I'll have Chris administer a late payment penalty. Got it?"

I nod. "One sixty-three by six o'clock."

He pokes me in the chest. "I just told you it was two hundred."

"The gift card has twenty-five dollars on it. Plus, the twelve in cash you took."

"I'm charging that to the expense of collecting." He flicks his eyes to Unrath, then back to me. "Two hundred. Do I make myself clear?"

"Clear."

"Chris, give him one last reminder."

Unrath steps back and delivers a right cross to my jaw. I collapse on the asphalt.

"Hey you kids! Get away from that car!" a voice shouts.

Samson and Unrath scram, while I curl into the fetal position.

"Are you okay?" the voice asks. It's Mr. Garrity, the school resource officer. Strange for him to be out of his office. He rarely emerges except to ogle the girls during volleyball practice.

"I—I think so."

"I wasn't asking you, Wimmer. I'm talking to my Mustang." Garrity inspects the car's finish. "It's okay, Baby. They're gone now." He glares down at me. "There better not be any scratches or you'll be in detention until next Christmas."

I stagger to my feet and wobble away as Garrity continues pillow talk with his car.

Welcome to life at Spiro T. Agnew Memorial High.

****

7:51 a.m.

I'm outside the west entrance, sitting under an oak tree, my back against the trunk. I grab a water bottle from my backpack to wash the taste of blood from my mouth. When I breathe, it's like someone's poking me with a sword. I worry Unrath cracked a rib.

More importantly, how am I going to come up with Samson's money by tonight? Asking my dad is pointless. He sure as hell doesn't have it. Sell his TV to a pawnshop and report it stolen? He'd be too drunk to notice. But I don't even know how pawnshops work. Make that Plan Z.

Would Susan Venmo the money to me? But Big Sister would want to know why. I don't like lying to her. But if I tell her the truth... Okay, that's Plan B.

Could I get two hundred for my laptop? By six tonight? Post it on Craigslist?

"Mike?"

It's Xenia Pendrova in a baggy red-knit turtle-neck top and a black skirt flowing down to her ankles. Never much makeup, but cheekbones sharper than a butcher's knife. Glossy brown hair straight to her shoulders. And eyes so purple they'd make the Ravens jealous.

We had Biology last year and dissected a frog together. That's the most we've talked. Her accent is enchanting, like a Cold War honey pot. Hungarian or Romanian. Bet she knows plenty about the Hapsburgs.

"Hi Xenia." I'm in no condition to stand.

"I wanted to ask a favor of you." She kneels beside me.

I almost tell her no, because I've got bigger problems, but stop myself. It never hurts to listen to a pretty girl. "Sure."

"My phone is missing," she says and adds nothing else.

"And?"

"And I need your help finding it."

"Did you check the lost and found?"

She narrows her eyes at me. "Really?"

"Just trying to be thorough." I shrug. "You don't need me. Just turn on tracking."

"I did. It must be off or the battery is dead."

"I'm not sure what you expect me to do."

Xenia leans a little closer. "You are skilled at locating missing objects. Like Shannon Green's charm bracelet and Roland Weinberg's clarinet."

True, I do have a reputation for being able to track down lost items.

She bites her lower lip. "My parents are quite strict. Part of the arrangement when they permitted me to have a phone was that I could not place a lock code on it. They could inspect it whenever they wished." A single tear wanders down her cheek. "After a few weeks they stopped checking, and I got careless. There are some pics on the phone. Pics of me. If anyone were to find them or spread them around, I do not know what would happen. But it would be bad. My parents might even send me back to Bălți to live with my aunt." She's sobbing now.

Nice try, but that's not going to work. I watched for three years as cancer ate my mom from inside out. I have no more time for tears.

As if she's reading my mind, the waterworks stop. She pulls a tissue from her purse to wipe her face and leans closer. The scent of violets engulfs me. She fiddles with my collar. "Maybe we could come to some other arrangement." Her breath is hot on my neck.

I've been pretty regular with Olivia Mitchell all year, and I don't want to throw that all away. But

Xenia is here, now. Her lips move closer to mine. She puts her hand on my sid—

"Argh!" I convulse in pain and toss her off me.

"What is wrong?"

"Wrestling injury." I try to catch my breath. It hurts to move, but it hurts to stay still. I'm in no mood for romance.

She sighs. "How about I pay you?"

My ears perk up. She must really want that phone back.

She fishes some bills out of her purse. "One fifty?"

That's a lot of cash she's carrying. Will Xenia's missing phone be my salvation? "Make it two-fifty."

"Two hundred."

"Two forty."

Her voice takes a hard edge. "Back home, when my family had nothing to eat, I would bargain with the vegetable merchants at the bazaar. No suburban schoolboy from America can out-negotiate me. Two hundred is my final offer."

"Deal." I reach for the green.

"No. Nothing until you find my phone."

It couldn't be that easy. "Okay, what am I looking for?"

"It is an iPhone 6s. The shell is the flag of Moldova: red, yellow, and blue with a coat of arms in the center. I lost it somewhere here at school. Last time I remember having it was at lunch on Wednesday."

"And when I find it?"

She pulls out a flip phone. "Text me." She gives me her number.

The bell rings. As she walks to the school, I turn my teenaged x-ray vision on her. The skirt is too thick, too long.

I shake my head to clear my thoughts and focus on the matter at hand. I have ten hours to find a two-by-three-inch phone on a forty-five-acre campus with sixteen hundred students, faculty, and staff.

***

9:55 a.m.

While Ms. Wisor drones on about congruent angles, I slip the textbook into my backpack. I'm half-leaning out of my chair, and when the bell rings, I explode from my seat. Though I'm three rows from the door, I'm first into the hallway. If I'm going to find Xenia's phone, I need Victor Yang.

If you want something at Spiro Agnew High, Victor is the guy to see. Looking for a little pot to take the edge off, Adderall to focus on the big chemistry exam, the answers to Ms. Foulk's French quiz? He's your man. Hell, Victor can even hack the school's computerized grading system and give you a perfect 4.0. All you need is cash.

I'm racing down the hall, knocking freshmen over like bowling pins, when Olivia comes into view. She's wearing a long-sleeved pink top that hugs her in all the right places, ripped jeans with specks of tanned flesh peeking through, and a frown that could ruin Mr. Rogers' day.

I stop, but only for a moment. I have to catch Victor before next class. "Hey Liv, what's happ—"

Whap! She slaps my cheek. Guess it's 'Beat on Mike' Day.

Her face is flushed red. She raises her hand again, but before she can connect, I snag her by the wrist.

"How dare you, Mike! Behind my back with the Russian girl?"

Gossip in this school moves at the speed of light.

I fake a smile. "She's Moldovan. And it's not what you think."

She raises her other hand and I grab that too.

Spittle on her lips. "You want to know what I think? I think you're a fu—"

"Sorry, Liv. Got to run. We'll chat about this later." In one swift move, I release her arms and duck the expected blow. I race away, and Liv launches into R-rated mode. I turn the corner, avoid plowing into the custodian, and screech to a halt outside the boys' room.

Inside, I find Victor in the far corner conducting business. He exchanges a baggie full of colored pills for a wad of bills from some blond-haired senior who smiles, stuffs his purchase into his backpack, and leaves.

Victor nods at me. "Wimmer? Don't usually see you in here. What can I get you? Molly? Term paper? Condoms?" He's wearing dark wrap-around shades like he's sitting at the final table of the World Series of Poker. His spiked black hair defies gravity. On his t-shirt is the image of the school's anthropomorphic mascot, Billy the Crab.

"Information," I say.

A gap-toothed smile spreads across his face. "Sure? What do you want to know?"

"I'm looking for a missing phone. It's got a red, yellow, and blue shell."

"A tricolor? If it has a coat of arms, then it sounds like the flag of Moldova. Which would mean the phone in question belongs to Xenia Pendrova or her brother."

"It's hers. You are unusually well-informed."

"Yes, I am," he says smugly.

"So, what about the phone?"

"I may know something about it."

"And?"

"And now we talk price."

"I'm a little short right now. Can I owe it to you?"

Victor's laugh echoes throughout the bathroom. "I have expanded my entrepreneurial activities past cash-and-carry, but not for you, Wimmer. Word is you're a credit risk."

"But if you give me the info, that will allow me to square up with Samson."

"Maybe. Not my problem."

"Hey, can we speed things up?" some kid standing behind me says.

I say to Victor, "Instead of cash maybe we can work out a trade."

"What did you have in mind?"

All I'm holding is a busted flush, time to bluff. "Christina Park." Christina is a senior, a knockout, and Assistant Captain of the girls' golf team. Clemson and Arizona State are heavily recruiting her. And of course, the Terps.

Andrew licks his lips. "What about Christina?"

Hooked him like a twelve-pound bass. "Liv's friends with her," I lie. "I could have her put in a good word for you. We could even double."

"Tonight?" His voice is filled with expectation, like a six-year-old on Christmas morning.

"I'd have to see if she's busy. But sure, why not?"

"It's a deal, Wimmer."

"Great, what do you know about the phone?"

Victor shakes his head. "After the date."

"This information is time-sensitive, Victor. I need it now."

"Not happening, Wimmer. Talk is cheap. You *say* you can get me a date with Christina. You're desperate and could be promising more than you can deliver."

"Come on," the kid from behind says. "I'm going to be late for English."

I turn, raise my hand, and make a fist. "Mr. Joslin's class, right? He's teaching Poe? How about I deliver the CliffsNotes version of *The Murders in the Rue Morgue?*"

The kid goes wide-eyed and scampers out the door.

Victor sighs. "I'm done with you, Wimmer. And don't come back, you're bad for business."

"Can't do that, Victor." I lunge forward and put him in a headlock. My ribs are screaming, but I can't let up. His sunglasses fall to the floor and in the scramble one of us steps on them and they shatter. I wrestle Victor toward the handicapped stall, kick open the door, and drag him in.

"Don't do this, Wimmer."

"Like you said: I'm desperate. You can stop it anytime, Victor. Just tell me what you know about Xenia's phone."

I force his head toward the bowl. With my foot, I depress the plunger. "You're getting flushed next."

His head is inches away from the water. "Okay! Okay! Alicia Duncan!"

I pull him up and slam him against the wall. "Who's Alicia Duncan?"

"Yesterday, she came to me with the phone. Asked if I wanted to buy it. Phones aren't my thing, so I told her no."

"But who is she? I don't recognize the name."

Victor shrugs. "Some tenth grader."

We have three hundred and fifty sophomores in this school. I need something more. I wrap my hands around his neck and squeeze. "What does she look like? Who are her friends? What's her schedule?"

"Spacer," he croaks.

"What?" I relax my grip.

He coughs and clears his throat. "She's a Spacer."

***

12:07 p.m.

My empty stomach rumbles like the engines of a 707 at takeoff as I enter the cafeteria. But there will be no relief, I have no money for food.

I work my way past the various self-segregated lunch tables: Jocks, Mean Girls, Preps, Skaters, Rockers, Drainers. The farther I progress, the less popular the cliques become. At the most distant table sit the Spacers.

That's our name for them. They call themselves the Valor Armada after the TV show of the same name. It streamed on some second-rate site I never heard of for half-a-season before getting cancelled.

To call them dedicated fans isn't right, more like committed. They cosplay characters from the show, dressing in uniform, mimicking the hairstyles, wearing prosthetics, and making their own 23rd century tech accessories. From a few phrases of alien dialogue spoken on the show, they developed their own full-blown language.

I walk up to a table where seven guys and three girls chat away in what sounds like Pig Latin at three times normal speed.

They either ignore or don't see me. I clear my throat, make the Vulcan Salute, and announce in my most solemn voice, *"Klaatu barada nikto."*

All eyes lock on me, including a guy who's wearing mirror contacts and what looks like novelty-gag rubber vomit on his head.

The leader, I'm guessing based on the number of orange triangles on the sleeve of his tunic, says, "It appears the Terran Amalgamation wish to initiate First Contact."

I sigh. "Sure. First Contact. Whatever." I glance to and from each of the girls. "Which one of you is Alicia Duncan?"

The leader asks, "Do you wish to enter into trade negotiations?"

These guys need to know that I'm not fooling around. "Look Jar Jar, I don't have time for your silly role play. Point out Alicia or things are going to Red Alert at warp nine."

Spacer Leader swallows hard, fear in his eyes, lips quivering. "In episode five, *The Dimensional Stabilizer*, production code 1x04, Fleet Admiral Chindlr is faced with a similar dilemma. But in the end, he upholds the princi—"

I grab Spacer Leader and lift. "I said point her out."

"Stop your assault!" A girl in a red-and-green tunic stands. On her head she wears a pair of bug-like antennas, skinny Slinkys with gold spheres at the end, that bob as she talks. "I am Sub-Adjutant Jeggex, but my human designation is Alicia Duncan."

I let Spacer Leader go, and he plops into his chair. "Nice to meet you, Sub-Adjutant. Yesterday, you tried to sell Victor Wang a ph—"

"Let us converse in private." She marches toward the empty corner of the lunchroom.

"Fine." I follow her.

In the corner, she faces me, standing at attention. Her lips are pressed thin. Silvery make-up on her eyelids and cheeks. Guess that's what they wear in the future. "What is your interest in this communications device?"

"Do you always talk like this?"

"Affirmative."

"I am trying to return the phone to its rightful owner. Do you still have it?"

"Negative." She shakes her head and the antennas make slow circles in the air.

"Where is it?"

"Negative."

I'm desperate, but I'm not going to beat the info out of a girl, no matter how annoying she is. "Sub-Adjutant, that's not an affirmative-or-negative type question."

She sucks in her breath, pauses, and blows it out. "In exchange for the location of the device, I seek compensation."

I spread my arms wide. "What do you want? Let me tell you up front, I don't have any money."

"I do not seek remuneration. I desire a kiss."

"A what?"

"A kiss. It is the process by which two Terrans show affection for each other. I am sure you are familiar with the concept."

This is like talking to a computer. "Yeah, I get that. Why?"

"I have observed that the primates of your planet are social creatures and sort themselves by hierarchies. The more elevated your position, the more status you acquire."

"Are we talking people or chimpanzees?"

"This is particularly important in learning annexes such as the one we attend." She relaxes for a moment and flashes the hint of a smile. "I rank you in the top quintile of attractiveness for male upperclassmen: tall in stature, blond hair, unblemished skin. A kiss delivered by you would increase my status, perhaps even the status of my crewmates in the Valor Armada."

I shake my head. "I don't think it works that way."

She shrugs. "That is my offer. And not some peck on the cheek." She taps her lips with her index finger. "Right here."

I look her over and the Sub-Adjutant's actually kind of cute: lively green eyes, button nose, slim. Plus, I'm already on the outs with Liv. What the hell. I wrap my hands around her waist, pull her close, and plant one on her. Her lips part and our tongues press against each other. She had grilled cheese and unsweetened iced tea for lunch. I lift her up to spin her around, but pain shoots up my side, so I set her down and concentrate on the kiss. Eventually, the need for oxygen requires us to break the embrace.

For the first time I realize the lunchroom has gone silent. No murmur of voices or the rattling of trays and silverware. I look around and the entire student body is staring at us.

The room breaks out into applause. Half the cafeteria chant: "Wimmer! Wimmer!" The other half cry out: "Spacer Girl! Spacer Girl!"

At their table the Spacers laugh and tap each other with their elbows. Is that the interstellar equivalent of the high-five?

With a smug look on her face, Sub-Adjutant Jeggex says, "Told you."

"Actually, you were pretty good. That wasn't your first kiss, was it?"

She blushes, but doesn't answer.

"Now what about the phone?"

"I offered the device to the trader Yang because I believed he would tender a premium price, but he had no interest."

"I already know that."

"I was not the one who discovered the apparatus. I was enlisted as an intermediary, but when trader Yang declined to bid, I returned the device."

"Who is it? Who has the phone?"

"Gilbert Bourne."

"Who?" The name is vaguely familiar.

"He is only the finest DM in the entire learning annex."

"DM?"

"Dungeon Master. He runs all the Dungeons & Dragons games."

***

3:32 p.m.

At center court, Billy the Crab, six-foot tall and fluorescent orange, stomps on a helpless muskrat doll. The auditorium fills with shrieks of "Beat Mandel!" It's time for the school's weekly thirty minutes of hate, aka, the pep rally.

The Marvin Mandel Muskrats are our archrivals, so most of the student body has turned out and they crave blood. But as I scan the crowd, I don't see Gilbert or any of his nerdy friends. My eyes drift to the cheerleaders, lingering on the exquisitely identical Maxwell twins. With their unnaturally red hair and impossibly high leg kicks, they are way hotter than freshmen have any business being.

I wish I could stay and puzzle out which twin is which, but I need to find Gilbert. I slip out of the gymnasium, and cheers erupt as Coach Sullivan shoves the muskrat doll into a portable shredder.

I wander down the deserted hallways of the school, peering into empty classrooms. I'm sunk if Gilbert's left campus. I pause at the bronze bust of our school's namesake and run my fingers across the inscription: *Nolo contendere.* But that's not an option for me. Could I run away? Would Susan take me in? How much is bus fare to Seattle? Probably more than I owe Samson.

As I contemplate life on the road, a flyer on the bulletin board catches my eye.

"Dungeon Master Gilbert Bourne invites all with adventure in their hearts to join him on a quest filled

with glory and excitement. Campaigns begin every Friday at 3:30 in the library."

I dash down the hallway and burst into the library. At the front desk sits the librarian reading a romance paperback. Four kids are gathered around a table covered with maps, figurines, and dice. Gilbert, in a cape and conical hat, sits behind a partition. The other three I don't know. One wears thick glasses, the second has an unfortunate haircut, the third sucks on his retainer.

In a movie trailer narrator's voice Gilbert says, "As you travel down the passage, you observe on your left a set of stone steps rising in a spiral. On your right is a locked door, painted bright red. Words have been scrawled on the door, but they are written in an unknown language."

"Let's climb the steps," Nerd #1 says.

"No, I'm a thief. Let me pick the lock," Nerd #2 says.

"First, we should try and decipher what's written on the door. That will inform our decision," Nerd #3 says.

Gilbert continues in his DM voice, "A chilled wind blows down the passageway. An eerie voice demands, 'Who w—'"

"Who wants to brave the wrath of the Unreasonable Junior?" I step to the table and tower over the four.

Gilbert sighs. In a squeaky voice he says, "Dude, we're playing a game here."

I cross my arms. "Me too, Gil. I call it 'The Search for the Missing iPhone', and with you being the best crypt keeper around I figure you could be a sport and help me out."

"It's dungeon master."

"Whatever."

Nerd #1 says, "We seek the Crimson Conjurer's crystal chalice which allows him to communicate over great distances. That's sort of like a phone."

I make a fist. "Do you want to see how many hit points you can take?"

Nerd #1 slumps in his seat.

"About the phone?" I say to Gilbert.

"Don't tell him anything, Gilbert," Nerd #2 says. "Upperclassmen need to learn that they can't come barging in and interrupt our game."

I lean over Nerd #2. "I'm contemplating casting the Spell of Traction on you. The effect includes a paralysis lasting six-to-eight weeks. Do you wish to attempt a saving roll?" I pick up the twenty-sided die and bounce it off his chest.

Nerd #2 frowns and slowly shakes his head.

Nerd #3 says, "My flying steed requires an enchanted saddle in order for me to ride it. Would you be willing to consider such a trade for the phone you seek?"

I say, "I'm the living embodiment of chaotic neutral. Got anything in your Wizards & Warlocks lunchbox to counter that?"

Nerd #3 closes his eyes and rests his head on the table.

"Okay," Gilbert says. "Obviously the game's not moving forward, until we resolve this. But what makes you think you can come in here and demand that I just hand over my phone?"

"I don't want *your* phone. I want the phone that Sub-Adjutant Jeggex returned to you."

A look of surprise on his face. "Oh, that phone. That's completely different."

"Glad I was able to clear that up. Now hand it over."

"I can't."

I pick up the screen and rip it in half. "I think I can supply the proper motivation to change your mind."

Gilbert shakes his head. "I didn't say *I won't*. I said *I can't.* I no longer have the phone."

I sigh. The hunt never ends. "Who has it?"

"Samantha Brahms."

"Samantha Brahms?" My breath catches in my throat like tar.

"Samantha Brahms?" the three nerds say in unison.

Gilbert nods. "Yeah, she asked me to try and sell it, but what do I know about that stuff, so I tasked Jeggex."

"Samantha Brahms asked *you?*" Nerd #2 says.

Gilbert nods. "I thought I was going to pass out when she started talking to me. She had on this green shirt and these tight jeans..."

Samantha Brahms: Head Cheerleader, hottest girl in school, and once upon a time, my best friend.

***

4:11 p.m.

My footsteps echo as I walk across the gymnasium floor. Pep rally is over. Pompom residue, bits of sparkly green and gold, litter the court. On the bleachers the cheerleaders are arranged into yet another hierarchy. Freshman occupy the lowest rows and all the way at the top sits Samantha.

Before I can climb the first step, the Maxwell twins rise and block my path. The hems of their skirts ride dangerously high on their thighs. Green ribbons secure their shiny red hair. I suck in my breath and try not to get too distracted.

On the left Tori, I think it's Tori, has her hands on her hips, and stares at me like I escaped from the zoo.

On the right, Toni has her phone in one hand and raises her other as a command to halt. "Where do you think you're going?"

Perhaps I need to raise *my* status.

I nod in the direction of the top row. "I need to talk to Samantha."

"About what?" Tori sneers.

"I want to ask her to the Homecoming Dance."

Tori rolls her eyes, but Toni can't help but crack a smile as she taps on her phone. The phone buzzes a reply, and her eyes widen. She shows the screen to her sister who shakes her head in disbelief. They part, opening a path to the top.

"Okay," Tori says.

"Go on up," Toni says.

"Thanks. See you later, Tori, Toni."

"*I'm* Toni."

"And *I'm* Tori."

I climb the steps while the rest of the squad applies make-up, gossips, scrolls through phones, and generally ignores me. A couple of rows from the top, Sam's peach blossom scent fills the air. My knees wobble, and I can't catch my breath.

Sam and I go way back. She used to live next door. Biggest tomboy in the neighborhood, perpetually covered in mud. We did everything together. Digging up nightcrawlers. A killer double-play combo: me at short, her at second base. In the fall, Sunday afternoons watching the Ravens in her room.

Then her dad got a big promotion and moved the family into a seven-bedroom McMansion in some gated community on the opposite side of town. Too far to ride my bike and that was about the time my mom got sick. We ended up in different junior highs. The next time I saw Sam was when she walked into Spiro Agnew with curves and legs and her brown hair was now blond and bright as a supernova.

I sit a few feet away. She's got her head down, filing her nails, and checking the phone lying beside her.

Sam looks up at me with eyes as blue as the summer sky over Ocean City. She flashes her dazzling white smile. "Homecoming?"

I shrug. "No one's asked yet, have they?"

She laughs. And not the silly giggle like when we watched reruns of *Pinky & The Brain.* This laugh is mature, sexy, aloof.

"I'm going with George Thoman."

George's a tool, but his dad is loaded. Bought George a Tesla Model S for his birthday. In my head canon, his dad is a bagman for the governor.

"It was worth a shot, Sam."

Her smile disappears. "Samantha. My name is Samantha now."

I nod. "Okay, Samantha it is."

"You should have no problem getting a date. You're pretty popular these days: Liv, Xenia Pendrova, the Spacer Girl."

"You're really plugged in."

She grabs her phone and holds it up. "Head Cheerleader. It's a requirement of the position." She sighs. "Why are you here, Michael? What do you *really* want?"

"I'm trying to track down Xenia's iPhone."

Samantha shakes her head. "You should steer clear of her. I mean think about it, Michael. The Russians tried to hack the election."

"I don't think she was involved in that; she's from Moldova. But this isn't about Xenia, it's about keeping me out of the hospital."

Samantha ignores that. Maybe she thinks I'm joking. Maybe she realizes I'm not. "Sometimes I think about us. We had some good times, didn't we?"

"Yeah, we did."

"I miss them."

"No reason we can't have more."

Samantha sighs. "Yes, there is. I'm Head Cheerleader, I have obligations, responsibilities, expectations to meet. And you, Michael? I don't know what you're trying to do. Slow-motion suicide?"

"Samantha, we don't have to let others define us. We can do and be whatever we want. Susan says that high school is the biggest joke in the world, but the punchline is no one realizes this until they get out."

She sighs. "I always liked your sister. Where is she now?"

"Seattle. Working for Amazon."

"That's easy for her to say three thousand miles away with a solid job." She looks off into space. "You think because I'm up here I have any real power. If I tried to do anything different, I'd lose it all." She glances at the lower bleachers. "They're all waiting to pounce as soon I screw up."

"All I want is Xenia's phone."

"And I don't want to see you hurt, Michael."

"Then help me. Because I'm going to be hurting real bad if I don't find that phone."

She leans forward, runs her hands over my chest, and her lips brush my ear. My heart races and my blood boils. I flash on the life I should have. A life where Sam didn't move away and my mom didn't get sick. Where my dad's not a drunk, I don't owe money to Frank Samson, and I'm dating my best friend who's also the hottest girl in school.

"Leave it alone, Michael," she whispers. "You have no idea how dangerous she is. Just walk away."

I slip my arms around her. "Believe me, when I say I can't. If our friendship means anything, ever meant anything, please just tell me where the phone is."

She breaks the embrace and pushes me away. "Can't help you, Michael." She taps on her phone.

I breathe deep. I don't want it to come to this, but I literally have no choice. "Eleven Pole Creek."

Her eyes are a mix of rage and fear. "You promised never to tell. You swore."

"I'm in serious trouble here. I have to do anything and everything I can to get that phone back."

"Fine." Her voice is ice cold. She pulls a phone with a red, blue, and yellow shell from her gym bag and throws it at me.

The impact of the phone stings my palm. "Sam, I'm sorry."

She pulls out a mirror and applies mascara. A silent signal that this conversation and our friendship are over.

***

4:42 p.m.

I have less than ninety minutes to return the phone, get the money, and pay off Samson.

I'm ready to text Xenia when my curiosity gets the better of me. She always wears baggy clothing. She's not on any sports teams. We've never been in the same gym class. I'm dying to see what Xenia looks like under all those layers. A body to match her supermodel face? I must see those pics she's so worried about.

I take a notebook from my backpack. Use my pen knife slice off a bit of the spiral ring. I straighten it out like an unbent paperclip and use the end to pop-out the iPhone's simcard. Now that it's off the network, I can power it up and not worry about it being wiped or tracked.

I scroll through the photos with great anticipation, but get nothing but disappointment. A black-and-white cat. Xenia's bedroom. Ducks on a pond. Some clothing store at the mall. This is what she's paying me for? Did someone who had the phone delete the good stuff?

What about video? My heart beats faster at the prospect of Xenia in motion, her hips under those thick skirts. First video is of someone, her mother(?), cooking a stew. Next, a golden retriever playing fetch with a Nerf basketball. The third video looks to be from a football game. I almost skip on, but let it run. I know why she's so desperate to recover the phone. And I pray I have a solution to my problem.

***

5:19 p.m.

I'm outside the west entrance. In the distance our band is warming up. The lights over the football field flick on. From my right Samson approaches with Unrath in tow.

"Got my money, Wimmer?" Samson asks.

"Not yet, I have until six," I say.

"Unless your plan involves an angel descending from the heavens with my money in the next forty minutes, you're through. And I don't feel like waiting. Chris, take care of him."

Unrath cracks his knuckles.

I raise my hand. "Here they come."

On my left Xenia and her big brother Efim approach. He's sporting a mullet like he stepped out of a nineties action movie.

"This is your angel?" Samson asks. "More like the devil."

Xenia says, "Nice to see you too, Frank." To me: "You have my iPhone?"

I pull it from my pocket and hold it high. "Xenia's paying me to recover her phone. You can give the money straight to Samson."

Xenia laughs. "You are one naïve schoolboy. I have no intention of rewarding you. Efim, get my phone."

Xenia's brother is even bigger than Unrath. He grabs my arms and twists until the phone drops from my hand. Efim picks it up and hands the phone to Xenia.

"Tough luck, Wimmer," Samson says. "Chris, your turn."

"Wait! Don't you want to know why Xenia pretended to offer me two hundred bucks to find her phone?"

"Not particularly," Samson says.

"Let us go," Xenia says to her brother.

"No, you'll really want to watch this." From my other pocket I pull *my* phone and launch a video.

Xenia and Samson step forward and squint at the screen.

The time stamp is from last Friday. In the video, Enrique Donoso, our football team's placekicker, is shaking, tears streaming down his face.

Off camera Xenia, says, "You are going to do this."

"I can't," Enrique says.

"You can and you will," Xenia says. "Or I will inform I.C.E. and your whole family will be sent back to Ecuador."

"Please don't," Enrique says.

"It is easy," Xenia says. "All you have to do is miss when I tell you. It will not affect who wins the game. No one will ever know, and your family can stay in America."

Enrique nods. "*Sí*, I will do as you say."

I stop the video. "Not the risqué pics of Xenia in a bikini I was hoping to enjoy, but still quite interesting."

"Efim, grab it," Xenia says.

Efim steps forward and squeezes my hand until the phone falls to the ground.

Xenia picks it up. "And now you have no proof."

"Do you really think I'm stupid enough for that to be the only copy? I've got the video stored online and off," I bluff. "If anything happens to me, it will be automatically delivered to the school, the local authorities, and I.C.E. Someone's family will be getting deported, but it won't be Enrique's."

Xenia's eyes are wide. "And now what? You want money? Not for finding my phone, but for extortion?" Xenia shakes her head. "Once I pay, what is to stop you from demanding more? I would rather take my chances and have Efim attempt to beat the locations of the file out of you."

I hold up my hands. "Relax, I don't want your money. Your secret is safe. Leave Enrique alone, return my phone, and no one ever needs to see the video."

She and Efim converse in whispers. He nods his head.

Xenia says to me, "That is an acceptable arrangement."

Samson checks his watch. "This is all very irrelevant, Wimmer. You need to pay, and time is up."

I hold up my hand. "Wait just one more time! This video is of interest to you too, Samson."

He crosses his arms. "How?"

"Evidence of fixing games wouldn't be good for business."

"But I have nothing to do with it. It's the Russians."

"We are from Moldova," Xenia says.

"Whatever, Ms. Onatopp," Samson says.

I say, "Right, you've got nothing to do with it. But a lot of angry bettors wouldn't know that. They'd want their money back and wonder what other games were fixed. Probably more folks than Chris could fight off."

"I suppose." Samson sighs. "What do you propose?"

"Wipe my debts clean, and no one outside this conversation ever sees the video."

Samson thinks it over for five seconds, nods at Unrath, who uncorks a haymaker, dropping me to the ground.

"You got your deal," Samson says as he towers over me.

I scramble to my feet. "You could have just said yes."

Samson pokes me in the chest. "Just a little reminder that if the video ever surfaces, Chris is going to drop you off the Bay Bridge."

"No, if that video is ever released, Efim is going to cut you into fish bait," Xenia says.

"I'm glad we've all come to a mutual understanding," I say.

"Thanks for screwing up a good thing, Xenia," says Frank.

"I am utterly unconcerned with your shabby bookmaking operations," says Xenia.

I step back as the two get in each other's face. Frank makes like he's going to poke Xenia. Efim moves in front of her and grabs his hand. Unrath lunges at Efim. Efim releases Samson, wrestles Unrath the ground, and pounds him in the head.

I rub my jaw and walk away amazed that my plan actually worked.

***

6:23 p.m.

Eight minutes into the game and we're down seventeen-zip to Mandel. With no money on the line, I can't fake any interest. Instead I'm focusing on the Maxwell twins. I plant myself in the first row in front of them.

My tête-à-tête with Samantha seems to have increased my status. They wink and smile and flip their hair. Still can't tell who is Tori and who is Toni. I look forward to continuing my investigation under more intimate conditions.

"This spot taken?" Jeggex asks. She's lost the antennas and the silver make-up. She's in a gray Johns Hopkins sweatshirt, navy blue shorts, and bright white sneakers with pink laces. She's got a set of legs that don't deserve to be hidden beneath her Spacer uniform. Before I can answer, she sits, closer to me than necessary.

"Good evening, Sub-Adjutant."

"I'm off duty now. You can call me Alicia." She nudges her shoulder against mine. "Everything work out with the phone?"

"All settled, *Alicia.* No trips to the ER. And it appears my ribs are only bruised, not broken."

"Where, here?" She pokes me in the side.

"Argh— Ha!" My body convulses in pain while my tickle reflex kicks in.

"Oops!" Alicia's lips curl into a smile and my mind drifts back to our kiss.

"Hey!" yells one of the twins. Their arms are crossed and they give Alicia the evil eye.

"Someone's not happy you're here." I nod at the Maxwells.

Alicia glances at the girls and rolls her eyes. "Freshmen. Let's give them something to be really pissed about." She loops her arms around me, pulls close, and kisses me. She tastes like grape bubblegum.

When I come up for air, the crowd is chanting, "Wimmer! Spacer Girl!" We're more interesting than the game.

Alicia says, "Perhaps we should continue this in a less public venue."

"I know a place."

We stand, I slip my arm around her, and we head for a spot behind the bleachers.

THE END

ABOUT THE AUTHOR

James Blakey lives in the Shenandoah Valley where he writes mostly full-time. He's a three-time finalist for the Short Mystery Fiction Society's Derringer Award, winning in 2019 for his story "The Bicycle Thief." He leads critique groups in Harrisonburg, Charlottesville, and Shenandoah County. His paranormal thriller SUPERSTITION was published in September of 2024. When James isn't writing, he's on the hiking trail—he's climbed forty of the fifty US state high points—or bike-camping his way up and down the East Coast.

Visit JamesBlakeyWrites.com, sign up for my newsletter, and receive a free copy of "Do Not Pass Go…" Sleuthsayers.org called it one of their "Best of the Best."

Follow me on social media:
Twitter/X – @JamesWBlakey
Instagram – @JamesBlakeyAuthor
Facebook – @JamesWBlakey

If you enjoyed this collection, please leave a review at your favorite book retailer.

READ AN EXCERPT FROM SUPERSTITION

A mirror shatters. An umbrella is opened indoors. A black cat crosses your path. All omens of bad luck that no one takes seriously. But at Van Buren University when these and other superstitions are broken, students die.

***

Saturday 1:13am

Her headlamp illuminating the way, the college student trudged to the campfire circle and dumped another armful of sticks and leaves.

Satisfied with the pile, she rested on a boulder, her breath visible in the chilly air as she retrieved a bottle of water. To her right, an Adirondack 46er loomed. Above, a cloudless sky of stars twinkled, no city to drown their light.

Easier to try this at the nature preserve back on campus, but even at this late hour that risked awkward encounters with pot-smoking art majors or insomniac townies.

From her overstuffed green-and-gold backpack, she retrieved half a dozen copies of the college newspaper. She crumpled the pages, placing them strategically amongst the branches, then marinated the heap with charcoal lighter fluid.

She struck a match and tossed it. Orange flames erupted, blinding her for a second, enveloping her in a wave of heat. The hypnotizing fire reminded her of summer camping trips with her father. *Should have brought marshmallows.*

Her phone chimed. Five minutes until the new moon.

She pulled out the shrink-wrapped lamb chops, on sale for $9.99 per pound at Price Chopper. The student wouldn't, couldn't, sacrifice a living animal for the power she craved. Even the thought of touching raw meat filled her disgust. She slipped on a pair of latex gloves liberated from biology lab, then tossed the chops into the flames.

The scent of burning meat filled the air. She hoped to finish before any bears or wolves arrived.

She retrieved the blue textbook, turning to the marked page. Squinting at the diagram, then the sky, she oriented herself, zeroing in on Orion's Belt. A couple of moon widths to the east, she located Alpha Monocerotis.

Of course, that wasn't what the Picts called the star two millennia ago when they ruled what today is Scotland. No one knew their name for it. Almost all their knowledge had been lost. One scrap that survived: their high priestesses worshipped this star for luck.

No bars on her phone. Not a problem. The student pulled the folded printout from her pocket, silently rehearsing the spell. There wasn't a person alive who could reconstruct the enchantment the way the Picts originally spoke it. Her new friends on the dark web assured her that Modern English would work fine, as long as it rhymed.

The past few weeks, she experimented with charms and simple conjuring. Enough to prove to herself that magic was real, and she possessed the power to wield it.

The phone beeped. *Now.*

She stood before the fire, hand raised to the sky, pointing at the faint red star.

The paper rippled in the wind. She focused on the magic, emptying her mind of all other thoughts.

As she recited the words, all feeling receded, as if her consciousness left her physical form behind, merging with the fire, the star, the spell.

Goddesses of the Night, hear my plea
Bring Success and Prosperity
My offering to you, a favored sheep
A promise to you, I will always keep
To my endeavors great and small
I call upon you, one and all
With a whisper soft and a heart so true
I conjure Fortune to come anew
Bring me riches, bring me fame
And banish all my doubts and shame
I summon the forces of Star and Sky
To grant me Destiny that cannot die
By my will and desire so strong
This Magic now shall not go wrong

Bringing Luck to my life at last
So mote it be, this Spell is cast.

She became aware: clothes sticking to her sweat-drenched body, mouth dry, hair plastered to her head, heart pounding. She stumbled to the boulder, resting, regaining her strength.

An owl screeched in the darkness. Good sign? Owls were supposed to be magical. Or was that some Harry Potter nonsense?

The owl quieted. No crickets at this altitude. No sound but the wind and faint jet engines as red-and-green navigation lights hurried across the sky.

The student didn't look or feel different. No supernatural power coursing through her veins. No enhanced perceptions allowing her to observe a secret world. No ethereal light enveloping her.

How anticlimactic. What do you expect for $9.99 a pound?

No way to know if she cast the spell correctly.

No way to test if the magic was working.

No way to tell if this ceremony was a big waste of time.

Not waiting for any predators that caught the scent of the sacrifice, she doused the flames with three bottles of water. Buried the ashes with her collapsible shovel.

Only you can prevent forest fires.

She scoured the area, gathering any trash.

Leave no trace.

She slipped the pack on her back and began the four-mile hike to the trailhead. She stifled a yawn. At least it was downhill.

Thirty minutes on the trail and her mind was numb. Legs on auto. Step, step, step. Leaves crunching in her feet. Another three miles to go. All she wanted was to get back to her dorm, make a cup of hot cocoa, and crawl into bed.

Gack! A spider web across the trail on her face, in her mouth. She spit and raised a hand as the toe of her hiking boot caught a root. She pitched forward, losing her balance, falling toward the sharp rocks on this section of the trail. Arms flailing, she couldn't stop herself. In the darkness, her hand grabbed a branch, wrenching her shoulder, but arresting her fall.

The student righted herself, let out a deep breath, her palm scraped and scratched. Need to be careful. Could have broken a leg or worse. Been stranded with no way to call for help. And no one knew she was up here. Pretty lucky.

A smile spread across her face.

Pretty lucky.

"It works!" she shouted into the night.

***

SUPERSTITION (Book One of The Secrets of Van Buren University) by James Blakey and published by City Owl Press available as an eBook or paperback from your favorite book retailer.